# CROWN AND DRAGON

## BOUND BY DRAGONS BOOK THREE

ALISHA KLAPHEKE

# INTRODUCTION

This is a true series so you must start with Bound by Dragons, Book One, to enjoy these dragon riders and their adventures.

Some of the worldbuilding in the Bound by Dragons world was inspired by the Roman Empire, bits of Estonian folklore, and a tomato festival held in Buñol regularly. I always like to research what inspired my favorite authors' books, so I figured I'd share that info.

Remember, there is spice on the page in this book —about two peppers strong. Some of my books have that and some don't. I just write what I feel the story needs.

If you'd like behind the scenes extras, some free fantasy reads from me, and updates on new books, join my newsletter at alishaklapheke.com.

**Thanks for reading!**

# CHAPTER 1

# TAHLIA

On Ragewing's back, Tahlia kept one arm looped around Marius's fabulously trim waist. She turned to see how close the others were following. The wind was cool and held the scents of hay and last night's storm system.

It was nearing autumn; soon the order would head north to watch the coastline for pirates. But for now, Marius, Ragewing, and Tahlia were on their way to King Lysanael and Queen Revna's vineyard. There, they would be briefed on the mission to retrieve the artifact the king's note had mentioned. It would take place during a human city's tomato festival. Tahlia couldn't wait.

The rest of the Order of Mist Knights flew behind Ragewing in three sets of arrow formations, a stone's throw from Ragewing's tail.

Titus pretended to vomit from the back of his Spikeback dragon and then grinned at Tahlia. She smiled back.

Last night while packing for the journey, they had both taken three too many shots of Maiwenn's green-blood—a batch of highly potent alcohol that was common in the Gwerhune where Maiwenn was born. Definitely a poor choice of drink the night before a dawn flight. Fara had been there, too, warning them to no avail.

"Maiwenn had best watch her back," Fara had said last night. "If you end up too hungover to begin your secret and surely terrible mission tomorrow, I'm going to rip her arms off. You just started and you can't afford to slack on your duties and she should know better than to tempt you..."

Tahlia snickered thinking about her friend. Fara hadn't tried to come along this time because she was up to her continually raised fists in Healer training. The irony would never get old. The most fighty gal Tahlia had ever met was working her way to being one of the best Healers in the Realm of Lights. Fara had sent Tahlia off with a stack of notes labeled *The only way you will survive this adventure.*

Despite today's headache, last night's imbibing had resulted in a slew of fantastic jokes about Albus, who joined in with his usual self-deprecating comments. And they'd been delightfully entertained by Maiwenn's classic impersonation of Atticus lecturing the staff at the tavern about overcooking venison.

Maiwenn waved casually to Tahlia and Tahlia lifted her hand in response. Maiwenn's dragon, Donan, let out a short roar in Tahlia's direction, a sound she was familiar with now. He was very worried about Lija, his fellow Seabreak, and her injured wing. He'd even barged into the Healer's fifth meeting on the subject when they'd gathered in Lija's stall. *Let's just say a worried dragon is not super fun to deal with.*

Tahlia focused on her bond with Lija and spoke through her mind—a power that they had awoken with Fara's suggestion of eating a certain magical plant. The distance their communication could travel was roughly a day's travel, but the range varied. Lija and Tahlia's Energy levels, the weather, and the activity of the crystals in the mountain altered the maximum separation they could have and still talk.

*Lija, how were the exercises this morning?*

*Lady Fara is quickly becoming my enemy.*

Tahlia laughed. *You don't mean that.*

Lija's growl reverberated through Tahlia's mind. *I just might.*

*Nah, she's the sweetest evil genius in the world and you know it.*

*Hmm.*

*You sound like Marius.*

A reluctant chuckle echoed from their bond. *Fine, rider. I will go along with your squire's exercise plan. But know this: I'll be well and flying before she can pass her Healer evaluations, and we will put this horror in our past.*

*I know you will, Lija. We will get through this.*

*I will miss the beat of your heart while you're gone, rider.*

*And I will miss yours. Terribly.*

Tahlia's eyes burned and she blinked back tears.

Marius leaned left and glanced over his shoulder. "I'm about to call out a kite formation."

"Got it." Tahlia clamped both arms around him and braced her thighs against Ragewing's saddle.

She relaxed and let the power of the belt that the goddess had given her rise into her heart and mind. It was like stepping into a hot spring, warmth seeping into her and reminding her that all was well. They would get Lija healed. It would be all right. She hoped that was true anyway. The threads couldn't show her the future exactly, though they did point to the outcome of her immediate actions in the physical space she occupied.

The threads of fate, action, and what she liked to think of as willpower connected Marius to Ragewing, Tahlia to each of them and to the dragon riders behind them. Certain spots on the ground or places in the air showed possible movements of dragons and riders. Somehow, the magic the goddess had bestowed on her permitted Tahlia to understand what each woolen-looking thread meant. When she wasn't suppressing her power—which she did so as not to become lazy—she used it to decide what to do at any given moment. She didn't want any of her fellow Mist Knights to believe she was taking the easy way out. Though they had all shown her respect and dedication since the adventure with the monster, Katk, she didn't think she'd ever stop trying to impress them. They were such heroes. She wanted to be like them still. Fearless. Skilled. Undaunted by challenge.

"Kite!" Marius called out in his Mistgold voice.

The sound bounced off the clouds and through her body, warming her blood for the coming fight.

Only Marius and Tahlia would participate in the mission to retrieve the artifact, but the rest of the order had been directed to escort them. On the way to the royal vineyard, the riders were to take down a band of thieves ravaging the Gwerhune forest.

"Spotted!" Claudia called out. Her orange tail whipped around behind her braided hair, and her sunset-hued skin sparkled in the midmorning light.

Her Heartsworn let out a staccato call and Ragewing answered her. They had been in the same unit for years and were as familiar with one another's calls as well as the calls of their riders.

"I see them," Marius said to Tahlia. "By the river. Can you give me a count, either of you?"

Tahlia didn't know if Ragewing had answered inside Marius's mind, but she did her own count, tallying the group of wild Fae drinking and laughing by the silver thread of water.

"I've got eleven by my count," Tahlia said.

"Eleven!" Marius shouted to the rest of the Mist Knights. "Unit Three, take the lead!"

Ewan lifted his hand and nodded his bald brown head. His Spikeback, Angus, dropped and sped forward. He and the others in his unit—Lucius and Cyrus each on their scarlet Heartsworns and Brutus on his pale blue Spikeback—passed Ragewing like bolts from a massive crossbow.

"What do you suggest, Tahlia?" Marius asked.

"Send a unit to cut them off because they're going to run, of course. Then send another unit over the far side of the river to come in low through the trees."

Marius nodded, then lifted his fist. "Good. You're learning. Down, One and Two! Three, get out ahead of them and circle back as they flee from Unit One. Two, veer past the river and come back below the canopy! Full flame, but watch the woods for spreading!"

"Full?" It was unusual for Marius to call for certain death.

"I read the report on these wild Fae. You don't want to know what they've done to terrorize the simple folk in the Gwerhune villages. Death is too kind, really, but it's what we have been ordered to give them."

"Aye, Commander," Tahlia said, dropping any feelings she was drumming up for potentially understandable crimes of those in poverty.

Ragewing dove, and Tahlia's stomach lifted into her throat. He unleashed a blaze that crackled and snapped. The thieves swore and began to run, all of them crashing into the river and heading north—as the threads had shown her. They were fast, dodging fire and leaping over boulders that turned the water into whirlpools. Wild Fae were a tough bunch, well used to doing what they had to in order to survive the dangerous Forest of Gwerhune.

"Durniad will take you all down, you spoiled pigs!" a wild Fae called out over the splashing and the sound of wings.

Ewan turned, his purple-blue eyes flashing, and directed Unit Three around to cut them off. The unit's Spikebacks and Heartsworns created a wall of light blue and scarlet.

Unit Two appeared through the trees on the far side of the river, their dragons already opening their mouths to flame and their throats glowing. All units fired on the thieves.

Their shouts and curses cut off quickly.

Dying by fire wasn't a lovely way to go, but at least it didn't have to take long.

The thieves' ashes swirled down the river, and what remained of the criminals was gone by the time the three units gathered beyond the moss-cloaked boulders that framed the banks.

Everyone dismounted and began checking tack and dragons. Smoke curled from the far bank. The forest was catching.

"We've got it," Maiwenn said, hopping back onto Donan. They hurried to the water, and the Seabreak—the same cyan-hued color as Lija—used his finned tail to douse the smoking trees and brush.

"Did you hear what that scum yelled at us, Commander?" Silver-skinned Atticus smoothed the wavy hair between his horns, uncorked his stash of water, and took a drink. He offered the water to Claudia, who took it with a nod of thanks.

"I did." Marius's nostrils flared. "If any of the rest of you heard what he said, please keep it to yourself. It's to do with our mission and we should bite our tongues unless the king and queen release us to speak about it further."

"Aye, Commander," Tahlia said, the others echoing the response.

Maiwenn and Donan landed beside them.

A stronger warmth emanated from Tahlia's Weaver belt. Tahlia touched the magical wool. "Ow."

Marius glanced her way, a question in his storm-gray eyes.

"I'm fine, but my belt is really hot."

"Your fancy Weaver belt?" Maiwenn squeezed water from her hair.

Titus's brow furrowed in a perfect big-brother-protector type of expression. "Your magic worked up there, right?"

"Yes." The belt sparkled and the light brightened.

Maiwenn stepped closer. "Whoa. What is happening?"

The dancing light flashed. Tahlia shut her eyes against the white flare of it. When she opened her eyes... Her stomach dropped.

The belt was gone.

The others gasped, joining her in shock.

Marius touched her arm and studied her face. "Do you feel unwell?"

"No. I feel the same..." The warmth was still there, but this time, it sat along her skin. She untucked her tunic from her weapons belt and eyed her stomach. A faint red pattern showed beneath her navel. She ran a finger over it. It was smooth, but... "The belt is—it's inside my body now?"

Marius took a knee and grabbed her hips. He brought her close and his gaze peppered her stomach.

"I see its pattern. Yes. Definitely. Did the goddess ever mention this would happen?"

She held her tunic up and squinted at the markings. "No."

*Lija?*

*Yes?*

*Do you know anything about my belt? It just, um, disappeared into my body.*

*Ah.*

*That sounds like you know things.*

*I always know things.*

*Yes, yes. Please, can you tell me anything?*

*The magic has likely grown used to you. It agrees that you are its keeper. I wouldn't worry about it. Your power likely doesn't want to rely on physical presence or varieties in the spiritual plane to interact with its wielder.*

Tahlia exhaled. *All right. Thanks.* "Lija suggests that the magic has fully accepted me as its wielder and doesn't want to rely on physical something blah blah something or other."

"Your dragon talks like that?" Maiwenn asked, a hand on her hip. She blew her Fae-white hair out of her face.

Donan snorted above Maiwenn's head, obviously standing up for Lija.

"No, Lija is very well-spoken," Tahlia said.

Donan lowered his head and blinked at Tahlia as if to say he appreciated the comment.

"Commander?" Titus started.

Marius was still on his knee in front of Tahlia. She didn't mind his fingers on her waist.

"Yes, Titus?" Marius spread a hand over Tahlia's new inking of sorts and delicious chills swept down her body.

"If you'd like us to survey the area and leave you two some privacy to discuss this development…" Titus shrugged, his smile barely restrained.

Marius's eyebrow flicked upward and he glanced at Tahlia's face, a teasing light in his eyes as he whispered to her, "If I were king…"

He waved off his words and stood, his thumb running over Tahlia's wrist briefly as if to secretly say he wished they could have some alone time. Heat rushed through Tahlia's body and her heart beat hard. She swallowed.

"No," Marius continued, "we must move onward immediately. We will need time to go over our information once more before the royals arrive at the vineyard."

Titus bowed his head. "Aye, Commander."

The order mounted up and flew below the canopy, enjoying the sights, scents, and sounds of the Gwerhune, the mightiest of all the Fae forests. Oaks as large as King Lysanael's castle, Caer Du, reached thick arms to one another, pixies floating within their shadows. The pixies wouldn't bother anyone until after dark.

They were lovely but incredibly annoying little things. The indigo pines took over as they flew onward. Needles shook in the wind of the dragons' wings, and the trees' fresh green scent rose into the honey-sweet air. Tahlia inhaled deeply.

"You like it here, don't you?" Marius said over his shoulder.

"I adore it. It's gorgeous. And exciting."

"Very true. Perhaps we can go on a holiday and explore the depths someday."

"Really? Do we get any holiday time?"

His body rumbled with a low chuckle. "Not much, but a commander can bend the schedule sometimes."

Tahlia slid her hand down his side and tickled his thigh. "I love sleeping with the boss."

Marius's laugh shook her slightly as she leaned over to peer down. A group of moss deer bounded over yellow and green mosses that matched their pelts and the growth that sprang from the buck's wide antlers. A tangle of roots boasted a cluster of towering pink flowers that grew in a long braid.

"We could bed down right there," Tahlia said, pointing.

Marius glanced down and growled approvingly.

Tahlia smiled and held him tightly. He didn't care about the flowers—she knew that—but despite his grouchy exterior, he was always kind about what she found lovely and enjoyable. As long as it wasn't something terribly reckless.

Would they be able to have some fun during this upcoming mission or would it be all risk and danger? In a perfect world, there would be a balance of both. After all, she didn't join the order to sit around knitting and oohing over flowers.

# CHAPTER 2
# MARIUS

The vineyard extended from the manor house into the rolling hills like a deep green wave. The flickering light of the workers' lanterns bobbed like fireflies and Marius felt silly for wishing he and Tahlia were only here for a holiday.

"Come on, slow poke!" Tahlia waved at him from the third row of grapevines, where she was dropping another cluster of wine grapes into the basket looped over her arm. "We have to beat Waith!"

It was tradition that every soul on the grounds during early fall join in on the harvesting. Marius didn't mind it one bit. This was honest work—and a calming break from the stress of dragon rider business. He wished the rest of the order could have stayed with them, but they were needed for tasks in the mountains. Training and keeping the occasional troll out of the high altitude villages would keep them busy in this fine weather.

Marius stalked over to Tahlia and took the vine knife from her outstretched hand. Her shining eyes reflected the lanterns' light and the glow of the moon. "First, you are so beautiful it hurts. Second, we don't have a chance against Master Waith, seeing as he has been running a vineyard since before either of us was born."

Tahlia had frozen, a grin lifting one edge of that pouty mouth he longed to devour like a decadent sweet. "I love it when you use so many words at once. It's as rare as unicorns, my love."

He growled at her and turned back to the vines.

She snickered and eased the basket into the leaves to catch the grapes he cut free. Master Waith, a male with fair skin, waved a hand at them, the two stripes of gray-white in his dark hair like the imprint of former horns.

"They will be here in the morning! Just heard." Waith nodded toward a slim lad leaving the vineyards and heading toward the stables. A messenger, Marius guessed.

"So we have all night off," Tahlia said, glancing at Marius from the corners of her painfully alluring eyes.

Marius's body heated, and he shook his head at himself as he adjusted his trousers. His mate could have ordered him to do literally anything when she looked at him like that.

"Seems so," he said, his voice rougher than he'd meant it to be. His tone didn't appear to dampen her spirits, thankfully.

"I think we should visit this exact spot after everyone has gone to bed."

He eyed the ground at their feet. Soft grasses had been pressed low during the harvest work, and blue-green moss laced a patch of earth here and there. Looking back at Tahlia, he nodded.

"Agreed."

She snorted a laugh. "You make it sound like we've planned some dark mission."

Using the full power of his speed, he moved behind her and set his teeth against the side of her throat. He edged the vine knife against her throat, though he kept the dull side toward her.

"I'll make it a dark mission if you wish it, little salty."

She shivered and rubbed her arse against him. "I do. I really do."

He chuckled and went back to harvesting.

They finished the row, and Waith called out for everyone to cease their work.

"Leave a cluster on each row for good luck!" Waith shouted.

"Aye!" the workers shouted in unison.

Happy conversation and laughter rose as everyone dumped their full baskets into the great vat at the back of the first set of outbuildings.

Most of the staff gathered at a long table outside. Dishes set with sauced chicken, piles of cubed orange cheddar, and fat slices of bread weighed the entire length.

Waith collected Marius and Tahlia and escorted them inside the manor house, where another feast awaited for the higher ranked staff.

A table had been dragged into the center of the main room. Platters of bright green apples and roasted venison sat beside flagons of dark wine. Round cottage loaves baked with the vineyard's mark steamed, fresh from the ovens behind the house. Varied wheels of cheese dotted the table as well as bowls of what appeared to be grape preserves.

Tahlia clasped her hands and sighed, her head tilting to one side. "Sorry, Marius, but I'm leaving you for this table. I mean, there is so much cheese."

He shot her a look and she stood on tiptoe and kissed his cheek. Thankfully, Waith and the other workers were too busy filling crockery with wine and singing harvest songs to notice or care about Tahlia's lack of propriety.

"We truly should go over the mission details as soon as we finish here."

"You aren't suggesting we skip this feast, are you?" She gazed at him like he had told her someone died.

"No, I don't wish to be rude to the household."

Tahlia put the back of her hand to her forehead. "Oh, thank the gods!"

"After we eat. Did you read the lines about Ragewing's position while we infiltrate the city, the location and purpose of the safe house inside city walls, and about our contacts both in the city streets and in the fortress?" he whispered.

He tried not to notice the way the soft skin under her jaw pebbled when his breath skirted over her flesh.

"I read the entirety four times. Ask me anything, Commander."

"Very good." He started to throw her a difficult query, but Waith's voice cut him off.

Those gathered for the smaller feast inside the house had at last stopped yowling like pups under a full moon.

"Please sit and let us talk about the first time you tasted one of the king and queen's vintage, Commander Marius, Lady Tahlia."

The talk went on and on, but Marius wasn't so uptight as to break the conversation to continue checking on Tahlia's memory. He kept his tongue and enjoyed the bites she fed to him.

"And this cheese is called sunlight. Can you even

imagine?" She tucked a sliver into his mouth. "What's it taste like?"

He chewed, savoring the flavor despite the fact that he felt foolish eating from his mate's hand the night before a mission briefing and in full view of the king and queen's staff.

"You're too slow. I'm trying it on my own." Tahlia sliced another bit of the sunlight cheese and popped it between her lips. She moaned like, well, like she wasn't just eating food.

"Gods save us, this is divine. The smoothness. The bright flavor!"

A female with curling hair and brown skin nodded approvingly to Tahlia. "My son made that," she said proudly.

Tahlia's mouth fell open. "You must be so proud."

The female grinned and refilled Marius's and Tahlia's crockery mugs. "He's only just reached adulthood and he's already working his way to mastery."

"Give him good wishes of undying love from me, would you?"

Laughing, the female walked off to join another female standing by the front door.

Marius pursed his lips. "Leaving me for a cheese-monger, are you?"

Tahlia patted his hand, then downed her wine. "At least you were defeated by the finest of competitors."

Growling quietly, Marius shook his head and finished his wine too.

WHEN WAITH and the rest of the staff had retired to their rooms in the house and in the outbuildings, Tahlia tugged Marius's arm until they were back in the vineyard. She had knotted her hair on top of her head and donned the linen shift that the staff had given her to sleep in. He wore trousers woven of the same type of linen. Both of them were barefoot, and with the crescent moon shining down on them, that fact only made him more aware of how wild he felt at the moment. His mate. A fine night. Time enough for mating.

Tahlia stopped near the vine they had worked on and turned to face him. "I've decided to wait on leaving you for the young cheesemaker until I've had my way with you."

He took her in his arms and pressed a kiss to her ear. She smelled like a goddess of pleasure—gently floral and as aroused as he was.

"Such a cruel mate I have," he whispered. "How will I survive you?"

She laughed throatily, the sound rousing his body as well as any touch. He laid her in the soft grass and braced himself over her, kissing her jaw, then the pulse point underneath. Her throat was silk. He licked and nibbled his way down to her collarbone while her hands tangled in his hair. She bucked her hips and rocked against his length.

"What if I slipped away and ran from you?" Her tone was teasing.

He was quite nearly shaking with need. "I would be forced to chase you, love." He set his teeth on her breast and growled, driving his hips forward. The pressure between their bodies poured pleasure through his blood. "You're mine, remember?" He gripped her hip and held her against him.

She moaned softly and shifted underneath him. And then she suddenly had a vine knife in her hand and was holding it to his throat.

"You will let me run, darling." Her gaze was taunting and absolutely the most desirable look she'd ever given him.

He eased away from her body a fraction.

She was up and running, laughing quietly, before his lust-hazed mind caught up.

"Oh, you are finished, little salty. I will hunt you and take you down in a way you will never forget."

Laughing again, she turned at the end of the row. He followed.

# CHAPTER 3
## TAHLIA

Tahlia hid behind the stand of maples near the first rows of vines. The bark was cool and soft to the touch. She leaned around to see how close he was.

Her heart stuttered. Just a fraction of his face and body was visible behind the grapevines. A low, quiet growl emanated from him. A shiver of delight ran through her. This dangerous fully Fae male with the vicious fighting prowess and the golden heart of a dragon was her mate. She had to keep reminding herself because it seemed too wonderful to be true.

And for some reason, she absolutely adored how frightening he looked right now. Her body melted with want—knees weakening and breasts drawing taut.

She fled her cover, grinning, and dashed behind the beautiful wooden structure that housed wine aging in barrels. The scent of the wine and the green aroma of the vineyards filled her nose.

Another rippling, spine-tingling growl announced that Marius was close. Tahlia took a trembling breath. She couldn't see him anywhere. Studying the shadows and patches of moonlight, she tried to see him. But—

Suddenly, she was up against the wine house wall with Marius behind her, breathing over the back of her neck. He had both of her hands pinned above her head and his other hand was rucking up her shift. Tingling showered down Tahlia's body from her scalp, down her thighs, all the way to her feet.

"Mine," Marius growled over the back of her neck.

He licked his way over her skin, and she gasped, heart pounding. With a quick movement, he twisted her shift around his hand and roughly shoved it above her waist, exposing her skin to the night air. The cool breeze was a stark contrast to the heat of his body. He pressed himself against her and the feel of him so ready to take her stole her breath. She was dissolving into pure pleasure.

"You caught me." She could hardly speak and her pulse was going a mile a minute.

"Yes, and I will claim you now." He thrust into her and held her pinned to the wall as he shuddered with the effort of trying to control himself.

She loved that he got as riled up as she did. He slid back, then drove forward again.

"Mine," he snarled.

His teeth found the place where her neck met her shoulder and he held on, almost breaking the skin. A thrill buzzed along her veins and she nearly cried out. She bit her lip, not wishing to wake the entire vineyard. Shifting again, he set a driving pace, and the pleasure inside her built higher and more powerful. The way he kept her tight against the wall, the desperation in his breathing, and the way he nipped at her skin…

He released one of her hands, seemingly caught up and lost in the moment. She moaned as desire tangled with the love she had for this male, and her pleasure peaked. She reached back, wanting to touch his cheek.

"We are not finished yet, my mate."

Breaking away a fraction, Marius grabbed her and turned her around. He lifted her so that she could wrap her weak legs around him. She was hardly a person, completely spent with satisfaction. His mouth found hers and he kissed her softly, his tongue dancing over hers and his teeth nipping at her bottom lip as he eased his way into her once more. This time, he took her slowly.

"I would seize the moon for you if you wished it. I would burn the world to ash. Ask me anything, my mate, and I will see it done."

Heart swelling past the point she thought possible, she gripped his broad, powerful shoulders and let her head fall back. He pressed sensuous kisses along her breasts, teasing her nipples with the very tip of his tongue as he moved steadily. His grip was tight on her backside, and the feel of his large hands was delightfully naughty. Need rose inside her, a sharp crescendo, then she came apart as he worked harder, his hips slamming forward.

"Tahlia," he called out as his eyes shuttered. The long, corded column of his throat moved as he took his own pleasure, his jaw muscles taut and his fangs bared.

He was the most gorgeous thing she'd ever seen.

They found a soft patch of grass within the rows of vines and he set to tidying her shift. His gaze turned to one of approval once she was covered once more. Then he sat behind her, one of his big legs bent so that she could lean on his knee, and he began braiding her tangled hair.

His whispered her name like a prayer. "Tahlia, my love, my dark soul longs for the light in yours." He dropped a kiss on the crown of her head, the warmth of his hands and breath making her shiver and smile. "I hear your heartbeat, and I want to follow the poetic sound for eternity. Your ferocity in the skies and your love of life will always be my light in the dark."

His murmured phrases about her body, his love for her soul, and his respect for her clever mind charmed her into a dreamy sleep.

## CHAPTER 4
# MARIUS

Morning came too soon and Marius only wanted to keep holding Tahlia against him in this warm bed. He'd carried her inside last night and the feel of her in his arms was so perfect—he could never deserve this.

A knock sounded at the door. "Commander?"

Marius untangled himself from Tahlia as she stretched and grinned up at him. He kissed her as the knocking continued. She was so soft from sleep and he longed to bury himself in her and forget the world.

Tahlia put a gentle hand on his chest. "Whoever that is will break a hand if you let him carry on much longer."

He growled but got up, pulled on his trousers, and opened the door. A young male wearing the king's livery bowed. Marius knew what he would say before he uttered a word.

"The king and queen have arrived and they request your and Lady Tahlia's presence."

"Allow us to ready ourselves."

The fellow bowed and Marius shut the door.

"So what do we wear for this? Battle leathers?" Tahlia held up one of their bags, her nose adorably wrinkled. "The villager clothing Waith gave us? I forgot my fancy cloak."

"I think we should dress in the undercover clothing, and keep your weapons to a minimum. Leave your short sword here, but take your daggers. One in your boot and one on your belt."

Tahlia lifted the shift she'd slept in over her head and Marius turned away so he wouldn't be tempted to get them killed for disobedience to the king and queen due to more lovemaking.

They met the liveried fellow outside the door and started down the corridor that most of the rooms opened into. The rest of the manor house was noisy with the sounds of staff preparing for the day—the scrape of small shovels clearing soot from fireplaces, the shuffle and crackle of new fires started, crockery clunking on hard surfaces as morning beverages were assembled, and the conversation of those long used to working side by side. The lad led Marius and Tahlia away from the ruckus and into a receiving room of sorts at the back of the manor house.

The room had a higher ceiling. A large window on one end showed the sunlight rolling down the green hills. King Lysanael stood enjoying the view, his arms crossed and his face stern. Queen Revna was pacing, hands clasped behind her back. Their crowns glittered in the window's light.

"My king, my queen," Marius and Tahlia said in unison, bowing low.

"Please have a seat," the king said, turning to face them in full.

Marius pulled out one of the six wicker chairs at the long oaken table in the center of the room and motioned for Tahlia to sit. She did so and he settled himself in the one beside it.

"In the city of Midhampton, in the human's kingdom of Saxonion, there is a human male by the name of Durniad. Though the young human high queen and her regent truly rule that city as its in their kingdom, he has seized those in charge. Through violence, he has turned the city to his dark purposes. He is a known criminal, a pirate at times, and a man who would name himself a king of sorts. The human high queen has requested our help because Durniad has supposedly uncovered an ancient artifact sometimes referred to as the Invisible Crown or the Crown of Minds."

Tahlia's eyes went wide, and she traded a loaded glance with Marius. He took a breath and focused on the king again. He had heard of this artifact, but only in passing during his early schooling. The crown had been mentioned in a list of dangerous items gone missing ages ago in a sea battle. He recalled someone deeming the artifact the Crown of Sirens. But how was this their problem? The human high queen—called high due to the fact that some areas of the human realm were ruled by lesser queens and kings that were subservient to her—was not of age, so her kingdom was mostly ruled by her regent. Fae King Lysanael and Queen Revna had aided the young queen in taking down her horrible father. They had signed an agreement between the two realms to aid one another as needed in situations determined as emergencies. This must have been one such occasion.

Queen Revna faced them, arms loose at her sides and her human eyes unblinking. Humans' rounded irises always unsettled him.

The king continued. "He will watch the parade during his city's tomato harvest festival, entertain those he deems worthy of his presence, and then, crown himself ruler of Midhampton. Maybe more."

"The fact is," the queen said, "if Durniad knows what he's doing with this artifact, he can control the behavior of every human alive. Those with Fae blood are safe, as are your dragons."

The king nodded and fiddled with the torc at his neck. "After discussing a way to resolve this situation and avoid a mass of mind-controlled humans from ransacking their own lands as well as ours, we decided to put you two on this mission. You must keep it quiet. The human high queen and her regent don't want their ongoing agreement with us to become an issue in their kingdom. Many humans still look on Fae as monstrous and deceitful, so the fact that the human high queen works with us on occasion for the safety of all must remain secret."

Ridiculous. Humans were the ones who were experts in deceit. They were the ones who murdered innocents in droves if even a small sack of gold was offered.

King Lysanael continued, bracing his hands on the back of the chair opposite Tahlia. "Since you, Lady Tahlia, are part human, you can handle any straight-out deceit required to complete this job."

Marius's stomach twisted, but he wasn't sure why. Tahlia could handle this. They could handle this together. Then why did he feel sick at the king's request?

Tahlia gave the king a quick nod. "Of course, Your Majesty."

"But be aware," the king said, "we aren't certain how a portion of human blood will react if Durniad makes use of the crown, so you'll need to stay together in case Lady Tahlia's mind is swayed."

They didn't have to tell Marius to protect Tahlia. That would be as natural as riding a dragon. He looked to Tahlia. Did she approve of this? They really didn't have much of a choice because this was the king and queen asking, but if she didn't want to be a part of this, he would figure out a way to respect her wishes. She was his mate first, a knight of his order second.

Tahlia gave him a subtle smile, showing her willingness. He shouldn't even have wondered. If there was one thing his mate possessed, it was courage. She had enough for ten riders.

Tahlia eyed Queen Revna. "We would be honored to serve Your Highnesses as well as our allies, the human high queen and her regent.

King Lysanael stood. "Good. One last thing: to ensure stealth, you'll ride your dragon to the human realm to meet with the human high queen's Witch; after that, you'll continue on horseback. The Witch will provide a glamour potion so that none of your Fae attributes shine through while undercover."

"We understand," Marius said. "Any further directions outside the written plan?"

"I ask that Ragewing hunt in the Gwerhune and leave my flock here be." The king grinned.

Marius nodded. "As you wish, my lord king."

Queen Revna studied Marius, and he stood

straight, letting her see whatever she needed to in him. He would have to get used to those irises. It was going to be so strange and off-putting to see Tahlia with human eyes and his own reflection too...

"If I may," Tahlia started. The queen waved her on. "Did you consider my request that we include Lija's healing as part of the deal with the human court?"

They'd sent that request ahead of them, and Marius hoped the wording hadn't put them off. He had been rather insistent despite the fact that he was asking from royals who could do exactly as they wished and he had to do whatever they ordered.

Eyebrow lifted, the queen sighed. "We did and we ordered it, but I will tell you, that Witch is not keen on handouts."

What did she mean? "My queen?" he asked.

Touching his torc idly, King Lysanael pursed his lips. "The Witch, intensely loyal to the human high queen, demanded that the retrieval of the crown be completed to a satisfactory degree as deemed by the human high queen before she will lift a finger for one of our dragons."

"That's a bit rough," Tahlia muttered.

"But your dragon can wait for healing for a fortnight or so, yes? Or should we press her?" King Lysanael asked.

"I appreciate your concern, my king," Tahlia said, curtseying quickly. "I don't want to rock the boat between the realms if it's not an emergency. I believe Lija can wait."

"Good."

"Then it's settled." The queen gave her husband a look Marius couldn't decipher. "Your full instructions are in a sealed scroll in your room," she said to Marius and Tahlia. "We have had our staff pack the clothing our contact in the city provided, your belongings, and food, water, and coin for the trip. You leave immediately."

Tahlia traded a glance with Marius, then they bowed and curtseyed each in turn.

"As you wish, Your Highnesses," they said in unison.

Marius wondered how it would feel for Tahlia to cross the Veil for the very first time...

# CHAPTER 5

# TAHLIA

Riding in Ragewing's two-seat saddle, Tahlia gripped Marius's waist tightly. Marius had braided back his long, moonlight-hued hair. He glanced at Tahlia over his shoulder.

"I'm assuming you just want to hug me and aren't feeling fatigued and in danger of falling?" he said over the wind.

"You got it, boss."

"Lady Tahlia." His tone was a warning. "We are officially on a mission at this point."

She grinned against his broad upper back. "Commander," she said, correcting herself.

He touched her hand briefly, then adjusted his grip on the reins. "We're almost there."

Almost to the Veil. What would it be like in the

human realm? Would it feel different from the Realm of Lights? Would it look wildly different?

"I suddenly feel unprepared for this mission."

"Just now, you're feeling that? You're a few days behind, Lady Tahlia." His chuckle shook her slightly. "We know our orders. We will go over the king's scroll again as soon as we finish at the Witch's house."

"Tell me what you know of the human realm."

"I've only been a few times, but it is less lush than our realm. The air can be positively fetid. But it is mostly breathable. The creatures are different from what we have. No forest dragons, except those taken by humans. No mountain dragons either. But they do have a very small breed sentimentally labeled pocket dragons."

"The humans themselves... I hope they are like Queen Revna and me generally, and nothing like my father." A shudder traveled over her heart, and a longing for Lija burned through her veins.

"Humans are not worthy of our trust. There are exceptions, but..." A grumbling growl vibrated through him.

Tahlia frowned, chewing her lip. She wasn't sure she liked how he had stated that. "Good to know." She decided to change the subject. "What do you know of the Witch?"

"No more than you do, I'd guess. All right, it's time. Brace yourself. The crossing will feel strange."

Threads glittered across the sky, sapphire blue and rose connecting Marius and Ragewing. Ebony and azure threads linked her to Marius as well as the forest, the trees, the animals that scurried and leapt below in the Gwerhune. A prickling sensation started on Tahlia's nose and hands before spreading to her scalp, back, legs, torso, and feet. She hadn't realized she'd shut her eyes, but when she opened them, the threads were gone.

"They're not here," she said, feeling unmoored. She had already grown used to the thread magic that Mother Twilight had bestowed on her.

"What isn't?" Marius tapped Ragewing's shoulder and seemed to be speaking to the dragon inside his mind. They began soaring in a more southeasterly direction.

"The threads. My magic doesn't work here."

"Ah. I had wondered if that would be the case."

"And you didn't bring it up?" she asked, blinking.

"You are deadly, skilled, and brave without your thread magic. It's a non-issue."

"I had planned on kicking everyone's arse easily!"

Another chuckle shook him. "I'm sure you'll still get a chance to take some foul humans out. Even if we are meant to be undercover during this mission, such endeavors hardly ever go according to plan."

The forest below held a softer green than the Fae realm's Gwerhune. It was sparser too, with fewer leaves on the trees and fewer ground-covering ferns and flowers. It wasn't ugly—more like reserved. As if nature had to watch its back around humans, so it was keeping a lower profile.

They didn't have to fly long before they circled the Witch's abode. Trees that looked to have survived a fire reached new branches toward the sky, and a collection of Unseelie portal stones—thankfully closed by the Unseelie king a while back—dotted the clearing around the house. Of course, "house" was a pretty serious misnomer. The structure's walls were like a castle keep—solid stone and imposingly tall. Slate tiles covered the angled roof.

Ragewing landed, and soon they were rapping on an overly complicated door. An iron-worked raven descended the length of the oaken slab while gears clicked and shifted. The dramatic entrance at last swung open to show a tall female with globe-like pale eyes and straight hair that reached to her waist.

"Welcome, knights." Her voice seemed to echo slightly as if she possessed a power that worked in a way similar to Mistgold blood. No one seemed to know exactly what race the Witch came from. She was like the Druid who often worked with King Lysanael— a being singular in make and beyond the pages of historical scrolls. "Come in."

She stepped back and Marius led the way into the stone cottage. A cauldron bubbled over invisible flames in the middle of the cluttered main room. Green light shimmered over the ceiling's rough-hewn beams. A colorful tapestry showing a human farm graced the wall. In the image, Unseelie monsters hid in the trees along the border. Bundles of dried lavender, yarrow, mint, henbane, and sage hung from a row of hooks. Doors leading to other chambers hid along the dark walls. Beeswax candles flickered along a wooden slab-type table that stretched along the western side. Vials supported with wooden frames, a mortar and pestle, and numerous colorful bottles crowded the table.

The Witch's gaze felt like a press to the throat—a blade's threat, not a kiss. "I have your potions," she said quietly, turning toward the table and lifting two corked blue bottles.

"Thank you, Witch," Marius said, accepting one of them.

He spoke calmly enough, but Tahlia could tell his body was coiled and ready to attack if needed. Not that he would win. The Witch was more powerful than anyone except the Druid.

The Witch handed the second bottle to Tahlia. The glass was cool and the contents looked oily. Tahlia wasn't exactly thrilled about having to drink it.

"You know," the Witch said, "your Queen Revna took this same potion when she infiltrated your realm to assassinate your king."

Was the Witch permitted to talk about the royals' sordid past? Tahlia doubted she followed anyone's rules.

Tahlia shook her head. "Such a wild story."

Marius's features gave nothing away as he stared at the Witch.

"I have adjusted the potion because you," the Witch said to Tahlia, "were once dosed with mintbane."

"You mean ghostmint?"

"The plants are the same, though their size differs, yes. I created this potion with a lower percentage of mintbane and added more of my other ingredients so it is less likely you will lose consciousness while the magic takes hold."

Stepping forward, Marius looked from Tahlia to the Witch and back again. "Lose consciousness?"

Though her stomach turned, Tahlia gave Marius a *calm down I've got this* look.

The Witch glared at Marius. "You won't feel much pain at all, but humans struggle with such concoctions. Lady Tahlia already has mintbane in her system."

"But that was a while back."

"It never leaves your blood."

"Ah. Great." Ophelia strikes from the afterlife.

"Is there any chance of permanent damage to Lady Tahlia?"

"There is always the chance that the magic will do something unpredictable. I can't promise you anything, Commander," she said snidely.

"Of course. We understand."

"You don't because you don't know the Old Language and can't work runes," the Witch said, turning back to her cauldron and staring into the depths, "but I appreciate the sentiment regardless."

"Forgive me if this is inappropriate," Tahlia said, "but would you consider traveling to Dragon Tail Peak right away to heal my dragon, Vodolija?"

"I will not heal your dragon until you fulfill your side of the agreement with my queen."

"I'd be faster and more capable if she were healed. Even if she remained hidden in a forest near the mission starting point, her presence would ease my mind and improve my physical abilities. Don't you want the most capable agent working toward your queen's goal?"

"Sheathe your silvered tongue, knight. The terms have been signed and neither of us can alter them."

Sure. The Witch, arguably the most powerful being in the world, couldn't alter terms if it pleased her. Right.

"There are things you should know about the artifact." The Witch stood over her glowing cauldron. Steam blocked half of her austere features. "We have two spies inside the city. The one who will meet you at the safe house says the crown has been stored under Durniad's fortress. Traps await you; I have no doubt." She twisted, and with her long reach, she took a small leather bag from one of the many shelves.

Marius accepted the bag, then tied it to his belt.

"Sprinkle that mixture in the room where you believe the crown to be. The magicked dust will force the crown to show itself."

"Thank you," Marius said.

"The crown can flood a human's mind fully and the wearer can order those within earshot to do anything they so choose. Be warned. I don't believe it will alter your mind," she said to Marius, "but you," she said, turning to Tahlia, "must be on your guard. If you manage to take the artifact, you will feel the urge to retain the crown for yourself; its power is alluring. Even if no one knows you have it, people will be drawn to you when it is in your possession."

A shiver trotted down Tahlia's spine.

"Midhampton is packed with people," the Witch said. "It's not a large city, size-wise, so the inhabitants are practically on top of one another."

It was Marius's turn to visibly shiver. He was not a crowd enthusiast.

"Many visit the city due to the port's heavy trade business. A couple of strange faces shouldn't raise alarms. Especially during such a popular festival. Now, I advise you to take your potions at the arranged spot where you will trade your dragon for horses. The effects should last around five days. Maybe three. It's hard to say."

"What happens if our Fae features begin to show in the middle of a crowd of humans?"

"Perhaps pretend you wear an elaborate costume? That or run away very quickly."

Marius's eyebrow twitched. "That's not exactly a true backup plan."

The Witch shrugged. "I'm not the Mist Knight. You figure it out. Or we'll all die."

"How would that go exactly?" Tahlia asked.

"Durniad will don the crown at his self-made coronation. This will not be the coronation of a lesser king, of one who simply runs the city of Midhampton. No, he will name himself the ruler of all. Don't think it's impossible, after all, with the crown, he will control every human on this continent, and quite possibly those in the islands beyond. They will come for your people. For the gold. For the crops. For the joy of overrunning your realm with sheer numbers."

The hilt of Tahlia's dagger warmed her hand. No matter what, she wasn't going down without a fight.

# CHAPTER 6

# TAHLIA

Tahlia flipped her shoulder bag open and rummaged around, careful not to upend the potion bottle. Before they'd left the Mist Knight's castle, Fara had given her a bundle of letters, and it was time to open the first one.

Marius had his back to her. He watched a break of rowan trees where Ragewing was hunting for lunch. They'd reached the spot where a human contact would be arriving with the horses. So far, no humans.

"What are you up to back there?" he asked, glancing at her. "Is that what Lady Fara gave you?"

"It is." She lifted the bundle and wiggled it. The knot holding the tiny sheets of scraped vellum in a neat stack was tight and hard as hells to undo. She resorted to using her Fae fang, hoping the human wouldn't show up at that moment. Supposedly, they hated Fae fangs. Granted, it was more likely the mountain dragon would be doing all the frightening during the upcoming rendezvous.

The knot gave way at last and Tahlia unfolded the first note.

*DEAR TAHLIA*

*Yes, you DO need to stay away from the water inside the human city. You'll pick up a fever at the very least and/or an extra eye if you imbibe from their disgusting wells. Just watch. You'll see loads of folk with superfluous fingers and so forth.*

*OH, and I forgot to tell you that a southern herbwitch is coming to visit Albus. She is the only known one in the world and we are going to experiment with what our Healers know and her specific abilities. Should be interesting! Will probably end in someone's horrific death though.*

*HAVE A LOVELY TRIP!*

*Fara*

"WHAT'S SO ALARMING?"

Tahlia jumped at Marius's voice. She looked up to

see him studying her face like she was an unexpected roll in a high-stakes game of Tali.

"You're surprised a note from Fara is unsettling?" Tahlia asked.

Marius snorted. "I suppose not. What are we to watch out for this time? Errant Unseelie gargoyles? Possibly the end of the very world itself?"

"Nothing so exciting as that. A Healer experiment, and a strong warning that human city water is tainted with disease."

"Actually, that's a good thing to bring up. Some human cities have water as clean as ours. Others I've tried have tasted uncomfortably like feet."

"So if it smells of feet, go with wine?"

"A sound plan. How many notes did she send with you?"

"Enough for one a day for six days. She claimed we would die without her advice joining us on the journey."

Marius shrugged. "I'm glad we won't have to find out. We should be in and out of Midhampton in four days, by my estimation. Come look at this."

He unrolled a map of Midhampton and held it aloft. Inked rivers, roads, secret passageways, and safe houses showed clearly from edge to edge. Not an inch was empty of scribbles or drawings.

"Here is where we will meet up with Ragewing once we have the crown." Marius pointed to a clearing that seemed similar in size to this one, although it was far closer to the city. "Inside, we're to pose as members of the city's temporary guard."

"I recall." He had insisted she read King Lysanael and Queen Revna's mission scroll five times. She hadn't complained, but there were moments she wondered if Marius thought she was an idiot. But perhaps that was part of the regular mission process, to go over and over and over the information. The scroll had mentioned Durnaid's tendency to use elaborate schemes for his own entertainment. The crown would likely be found amidst numerous traps and there was talk of a labyrinth.

"Durniad hires numerous extra bodies to keep the peace during the festival," Marius said. "We'll head first to the safe house near Bodwin Bridge to dress the part."

Marius looked down at her and a wave of longing swept through her. She wanted his body on hers. Was there time before the human with the horses arrived?

He lifted an eyebrow. "I hate to disappoint you, but I'll not be dressing as a tomato for this mission."

"Murderer of dreams, that's what you are." Besides, he probably didn't know for sure what the uniforms for temporary guards looked like. He could be wrong.

The corners of his handsome mouth—a mouth she suddenly and immediately wanted all over her—

edged up at the corners, making her heart flip. Still holding the map in one hand, he smoothed a palm along her jaw and down the side of her neck. His storm-gray and slitted irises darkened as he leaned down to kiss her.

His mouth claimed hers, his tongue exploring the underside of her top lip and making her toes curl inside her soft villager boots. His hand slid around the back of her neck and his thumb hooked the front of her throat.

"So possessive," she whispered as he licked her earlobe.

"Do we have time for this, Commander Marius?"

He only answered with a growl as he burrowed into her neck, nipping and licking lightly. The map fluttered to the ground and he backed her up against a boulder.

Ragewing landed gracefully, his tongue darting across the tip of his snout.

Marius's eyes shut briefly before he met Tahlia's eyes. "Sorry."

Tahlia kissed his delicious jawline. "The mission comes first. I know that."

He held her hand, and they walked up to Ragewing. Tahlia exhaled, trying to let go of the desire rushing through her blood. She had to focus on the mission and prove to Marius they could do this even though they were mated fully now. She wanted to show everyone that they could be a mated pair and the best Mist Knights on the mountain.

"Good meal, my friend?" Marius asked him, retrieving and rolling up the map.

Ragewing lifted his scarlet head and a low, staccato growl rumbled from his throat.

"He says he saw the human and his horses two miles or so away," Marius said, looking from Ragewing to Tahlia.

Tahlia let out a sigh and pushed a fisted hand against the knot in her stomach. "Guess it's finally time to poison ourselves."

Marius chuckled darkly.

"Ragewing," Tahlia said, "how do you think Lija is doing? I can't hear her anymore."

The dragon looked to his rider. Marius nodded, rubbing his chin in thought.

"Ragewing says she is strong in spirit, though the challenge is one of the most difficult a dragon can face."

Tahlia said a silent prayer to the gods. Lija had to survive this. They had to heal her.

The massive scarlet dragon spread his wings slightly and bowed his head. Grateful to him, Tahlia smiled and curtseyed back, some of the knot in her stomach untangling.

Marius put a hand on Ragewing's neck. "Thank you for carrying my mate again." He tilted his head, listening to Ragewing in his mind. A laugh crept from his lips and he turned to Tahlia. "He says if you'd sit still in the saddle, the job would be far less anxiety-inducing."

Tahlia stuck her tongue out at both of them. She slipped her potion free of its leather holder, then she uncorked it at the same time as Marius opened his bottle. "Well, we need to move forward with our plans, right? I think we should human ourselves before the contact arrives with our horse. So he is less frightened of us."

"Agreed."

"Time to human." She lifted the concoction into the lines of sun that broke through the trees. "Bottoms up!"

Marius nodded, raising his potion, then he downed the stuff. She did likewise.

The potion tasted like regret and maybe deer piss? Super delightful. Ugh. She turned away from Ragewing and Marius, stomach rolling.

A warm hand found her shoulder.

"Are you all right?" Marius's breath tickled the hairs at the side of her face.

She realized she was on her knees in the dirt and grass. When had she dropped?

"I've been better, but I'll live," she said.

The world tilted and she swallowed, willing her body to accept the magic.

"Lady Tahlia, talk to me. Tell me you're all right. Or expunge it from your body and we will figure out another way to do this. I will go on my own."

Holding up a hand, she bit out her words. "No. Can't ruin mission." She did her best to grin up at him.

Nodding, he helped her to her feet. "Ach, you're fine. I see that salty little smirk."

His ears shimmered and morphed, edges rounding into a human-like shape. His skin dulled ever so slightly and as he blinked, his slitted irises became circles.

"So strange," she whispered, touching the cheekbone on the left side of his face as it lost its Fae sharpness and became less pronounced.

He was studying her like she was examining him. His gaze peppered her here and there, as if he was cataloguing the changes. "Fascinating."

"Do I pass as fully human now?" *Gods above, have mercy on me*, she prayed silently. Nausea swirled inside her. It was all she could do to keep from losing the contents of her belly. Dots swam in front of her eyes.

"You don't look well. And I'm not just talking about the human features," he said.

"It'll pass."

"We're not going anywhere until it does," he said in a tone that didn't brook any arguments.

"Yes, we are. I'm doing this for Lija, and I am not letting an upset stomach get in my way."

Ragewing snorted, then took off into the air. He flew toward the darker side of the forest.

Marius watched him go. "He says our rider approaches. Ragewing will hide himself to avoid startling the horses. He told me to bid you best wishes."

Tahlia smiled. "Tell him thank you."

A human with tan cheeks and light green eyes—and of course, his irises were round—rode into the clearing on a russet-hued mare. The human had two more horses on leads trailing behind—one dun with a star on his nose and one as black as night.

"The power of the wicked is nothing to those with hearts of fire," the contact said.

Marius lifted a hand in a wave. "Fire, we have." He put his fist to his chest.

Tahlia's stomach was absolutely stuffed with butterflies. Code phrases like that just made it all seem so real once again; she was a Mist Knight and she was on a mission. It was amazing!

The human dismounted. Tahlia could tell he was male from the set of his shoulders, but she wished he weren't cloaked and hooded so she could study his looks more closely. He had a snub nose and a heavy jaw. He didn't have the sheen to his flesh that those with Fae blood had, but other than that, he appeared pretty much the same. His movements were what gave him away as human. Though he was clearly experienced with horses—he dismounted easily and gathered the mounts like it was what he did every day of his life—his hands worked in a slower, less graceful manner. The strides he took to approach them, reins held loosely, were ungainly in a way a Fae would never appear.

Tahlia suddenly worried they wouldn't be able to blend in for this mission. Their movements would give them away, surely.

The contact gestured toward the two horses he'd brought for them. "They're good creatures. Biddable. Smart. Won't startle too easily. And they're trained to return to our place when you release them. Please do so before you come out of the tree cover near Midhampton. I don't want any would-be thieves trying their hand at stealing my horses."

"Understood," Marius said, approaching the black stallion. He picked a bit of clover from the ground and held it in his palm for the horse to lip up. "Has the festival plan changed at all?"

"Not as far as I know. Your in-town contact will know more. He has your guard uniforms."

"Oh, we had thought..." Tahlia picked at her tunic.

The man shook his head. "No, you'll have official uniforms."

Oooh, maybe there would be a really obnoxious pattern at least. Tahlia grinned and Marius glared at her like she was due for a scolding.

"As for the parade," the contact went on, oblivious

to Tahlia and Marius's silent discussion, "for now, it seems it will begin at Bodkin Bridge. It'll be hard to miss. They always drape it in banners. On the far side. It will wrap in an easterly direction through the oldest parts, down near the docks, then curve back to the fortress, near the other side of Bodkin. There will be stages set up along the parade route and traffic will stop to allow for the customary dances and competitions."

"What do those involve?"

"The dances are performed by anyone willing. Sometimes, an official or guild leader will push someone on stage. It's tradition. The competitions are preplanned. Jugglers tossing tomatoes. Folks balancing on one another's shoulders to build human towers. Comedic acts that the crowd votes on by cheering. That sort of nonsense."

Marius gave the man a nod that said he liked how he didn't approve of silly things like that. Tahlia bit her lip to keep from snickering. Grouchy old things, they both were.

"Meet your contact at the safe house. Dress the part. Uniforms are hidden in an armoire in the kitchen. Enter the parade. Blend in. Head to the fortress as soon as you're able and we have a couple of inside folks there to help you out. Better you than me, I'll tell you that. I don't know how you're going to find an invisible artifact."

"We have our ways." Marius led the stallion a few steps away and released his reins so he could nibble at the tall grass.

"I leave you to it, then." The man handed the dun's reins to Tahlia, then he mounted up. "Best of luck to you!" he called out as he rode away.

Tahlia watched him until he was out of sight.

"I'm trying not to be jealous of a human male." Marius climbed onto his horse's saddle.

"It's only curiosity."

"I understand." The sides of his mouth lifted a fraction like he was trying to smile at her, but his eyes burned with worry or confusion—she wasn't sure.

They rode into the woods. Soon, they'd be entering a human city. As they sped through the shadows of fat-trunked beech trees and around tangles of thorn bushes, Tahlia made herself breathe slowly in and out. Excitement and curiosity made it incredibly difficult to keep from asking the horses to gallop even faster than they already were.

CHAPTER 7

# TAHLIA

The city of Midhampton boasted a fine arched entryway flanked by two tower guard houses—more security than most Fae towns and cities, but not as many as the Mist Knights' castle or Caer Du, the heart of the Fae realm. A long string of humans made their way under the archway, stopping now and then to answer the guards' questions. A group of minstrels in silks carrying lutes, pipes, and drums were ushered through with a laugh from a heavily bearded guard. Carts holding everything from crates of chickens to trunks overflowing with textile goods rolled into the city, mules and horses tugging them along at the behest of merchants and their families. Conversation and giggling rose in the cool, briny air to mix with the squawk of sea birds.

The cobblestones beneath Tahlia's boots weren't

made of the same sturdy rock as the roads in the Realm of Lights. This rock was sandy and gritty under her step. One would slide on this surface if one came to an abrupt stop. A good thing to remember if it came to fighting.

Marius's warm presence at her back made Tahlia even bolder as their turn to answer the guards' questions arrived.

"Business or pleasure?" The guard had a low voice, and his mustache did a pretty great job at muffling what sound did attempt to come out.

"Pleasure," Tahlia said before Marius could attempt the word and ruin the mission with his inability to sound like he was about to have some fun.

The guard glared at Marius, who forced a grin. A grimace? Not sure what that was.

"Where in the city will you stay?" That mustache was almost broom-like. "I hope you don't think you can just wander in and find lodgings anywhere. And there's no sleeping on the street."

Marius nodded. "We have a room at The Stag and Pheasant."

"Oh, fine place, that," the guard said, stepping back to let them pass.

The crowd jostled Tahlia as they made their way under the arched gateway. An entertainer dressed in red stripes grinned at an incredibly tall man who carried a sack. The top of the corn dolly stuck out from the sack. Two carts of ale barrels lumbered past, nearly squashing Tahlia's foot. Marius pulled her back.

"Watch yourself, now."

"There's so much to look at. And they look so strange." Humans weren't ugly, but they didn't have the grace of Fae. It hadn't just been their horse contact; they were all a bit lumbering. They appeared softer, and honestly, their smiles appeared more genuine. "I didn't expect to like the look of them," she said quietly.

The surrounding noise of parents instructing children and excited conversation amongst merchants lugging their wares made it plenty safe for her to speak to Marius.

He leaned down, his lips grazing her ear. "You have a kind and generous spirit, and I can't fault you for that."

Human pirates had killed Marius's sister. She truly hoped he didn't hate all of them because of that. Would Marius tell her if he felt differently? Even if he wished he didn't?

"If we end up needing the others, how will we signal them?"

"I would need to get close enough to Ragewing to communicate a message that he would fly back to Dragon Tail Peak."

"Can you hear him now?"

Marius squinted as they walked. "No, we're too far,

I guess. I have noticed the ability is spotty outside the Veil."

The main thoroughfare rose like a scared cat's back, and the city opened up below. Orange tiles lay in neat lines along rooftops, the East Border River slid through the buildings and roads, and the scent of roasted meat and baking bread perfumed the air. Large carts filled with tomatoes sat at almost every intersection, ready for the insane ritual of tossing the red vegetables—or fruits, really—until pulp swamped ankles and dribbled into open doorways. Numerous walkways arched over crossway paths and small bridges slanted across Midhampton. One bridge in particular commanded attention. Lined with flapping banners in every shade of red, the bridge that stretched wide over the river seemed to be welcoming everyone to the festival.

Tahlia bounced on her heels before she continued onward to catch up to Marius. "We should have practiced the telepathic chatting with varying distances before this mission."

"We had no time for a proper exploration of the limits and with your Lija still injured—"

A woman pushed through the crowd and fell onto Marius with a laugh that stank of ale.

"Hello, beautiful," she said to him, her words slurring. "Want a little pre-festival fun?"

Marius gently but firmly eased her off of him. "No,

good woman. I have a companion." He tilted his head toward Tahlia.

The stream of people pushed them forward. The woman disappeared in the crowd, her hand waving above a family dressed in red for the parade. Marius took Tahlia's elbow and ushered her toward a narrow side street.

The excitement of the city's inhabitants and visitors zipped through Tahlia, and she felt incredibly hopeful. They would enjoy the festival, nab the invisible crown, and be home before Fara's Healer evaluation for sure. Tahlia didn't want to miss supporting her on her first test with Albus.

The crowd pulled them along, and soon a bridge—made of rose-hued stone that glittered in the sun—spread out, arching above the masses. The street they were on passed under Bodwin Bridge on the southern side, with the river dashing about in its banks to their left. They came out on the far side, and a shout hammered the air.

"You with the white hair, halt in the name of King Durniad!"

Tahlia's heart stilled and she gripped Marius's wrist. "The Witch's potion should've been set to hide that pretty mane of yours."

## CHAPTER 8
## MARIUS

It was a city guard. There were humans with hair nearly as white as Marius's, but perhaps this fellow had specific issues with Fae and was more prone to jump at any chance to find one and give one trouble. Even when the Fae helped them, some humans possessed an unbreakable hate for Fae. The guard's tassels indicated officer-level ranking as per the mission details. He was alone, so they could likely evade him if he was indeed shouting at them.

"Should we run?" Tahlia whispered.

"Not yet. It could be anything. Stay calm."

She shielded her eyes from the blazing sun. "I can't tell if he is looking this way or not."

"I don't think so."

"You're sure?" she asked.

"Not yet."

"I don't like it when you're not sure. You're always sure."

"That's incorrect."

"See? You're certain I'm wrong." Her lovely fingers left his wrist, and he mourned the loss like a lovesick youngling.

The guard was parting the crowd and coming their way.

He growled quietly. "We need to work our way out of here."

"Got it." Tahlia shot to the right, going across the crowd.

It was more obvious, but it was the fastest way to shift their direction. Conversations and the general noise of the people started up again, but the guard had his gaze set on Marius and he wasn't slowing, his body parting the crowd like a prow on the water.

Tahlia was already taking a turn to join the throng walking across the bridge on the upper level, over the place where they'd just been. Marius trailed her, carefully easing folks aside as he went. This was easier for Tahlia because she was so small. She was halfway across the bridge by the time he reached her.

It was like her head was on a swivel. "Is he following us? Where is he?"

"Look straight ahead. Aim for the second street to the right. We will cross the river again at the next bridge."

"Aye, aye." She winked at him and kept on.

Finally, they were moving in sync with the crowd. The bridge sloped down to the street once more, and they skirted their way along the edges of the people. An open door beckoned from a basketweaver's shop.

"Here. This is better."

He put a hand to the small of her back and immediately wished he hadn't because the feel of her shape caused his blood to flow away from his brain, heading south. He followed her into the shop.

"Oh, I love these!" She picked up a basket and stared at it like it was a lost treasure found.

"Do you?" The shopkeeper clasped her hands. Her eyes shone with delight. "It's my newest design."

The back door was clear, straight back. He cut past Tahlia and the basketweaver and into the dark of the back of the shop. Two small boys looked up at him from the corner where they were sorting what looked like the reeds that grew on the seaside. Marius whistled once, quick and high, a sound Tahlia would notice, but most would excuse as street noise filtering in.

Tahlia laughed at something the shop woman said, and she hurried back to join him. They were out the back door in seconds.

"What did you tell her?"

"That your ex was out front."

Marius snorted and led her over the cobblestones

and toward the road to the next bridge, if they needed to use it. But if they found the safe house first, they would just go there.

Only a small group of elder humans and a skinny dog walked down this side street. The turn was clear of guards so far. They slipped down the road, and at last, the blue-painted door of the safe house appeared at the end of a more crowded lane. In front of the door, a wooden gate circled a tiny garden. Marius pushed it open and Tahlia hurried through and tried the door.

"Locked," she said quietly as she smiled at a passerby. She was handling this well, acting casual and masking their need to work quickly.

With a glance over his shoulder to check for the city guard or anyone who seemed too curious about them, Marius rammed his shoulder against the painted oak. He grunted as the door banged open. They rushed inside. He shut the slightly damaged door behind them.

"Where are the uniforms again?" Tahlia asked. "I can't remember what he said about that."

"Kitchen. It's always the kitchen for some reason. Perhaps because no one tends to search kitchens. I'll check that the house is clear first. You go on." He stalked down the narrow hallway that led to two bedchambers. Nothing.

"All clear," he called out.

"I found cheese!" Tahlia's voice echoed down the hallway.

The city cottage's kitchen was small and in need of cleaning, but the armoire was exactly where the contact said it would be—against the wall beside a window that looked out on a shared inner courtyard choked by weeds that nicely blocked the kitchen from view. Tahlia was digging through a smaller cabinet and shoving bits of yellow cheese into her mouth.

"You should eat some," Tahlia mumbled over a mouthful. "We'll need energy for this mission. Plus, it's delicious."

"I have no time for cheese. The contact will be here soon. We must be ready."

"It's like you hate yourself," Tahlia muttered, joining him at the armoire.

He paused, eyeing the windows to be sure the city guard hadn't found his way here. Tahlia tugged the armoire doors open, and a mass of fur flew out.

Heart hammering, Marius shoved his way in front of her, his dagger unsheathed and ready. Tahlia grabbed his hand and pushed his weapon down.

"They're kittens!" she cried.

Blinking, Marius looked at the armoire, the kitchen floor, and then at Tahlia. Furry rodents crawled everywhere. And Tahlia was holding one and cooing at it.

"Aren't they adorable? Sweet little darling." She kissed the cat she was holding.

"Get that thing off of you. It could have one of a thousand diseases and we have work to do."

"Fara would agree, but alas, I do not." Tahlia stroked the cat's black fur and bent to pick up another of the small menaces.

One striped creature began climbing Marius's trousers, and he plucked it off. He held it aloft to study it. "They definitely have fleas, as well as claws as sharp as a youngling dragon's."

Laughing, Tahlia took the striped nightmare from him and added it to the collection currently on her shoulders and in the crook of her arm.

Marius shook his head and growled. "Shoo the small demons away. We have work to do."

"Demons." She laughed harder. "Your face right now is making this entire mission so worthwhile."

He gritted his teeth and turned back to the armoire. Lifting a basket, he searched for the uniforms. Another furred devil shot out of the shadowed back corner of the cabinet and latched onto his tunic. It smelled like a sewer rat. He detached the beast with careful movements.

"You're treating that demon awfully carefully," Tahlia said snidely.

A growl echoed from him as he passed the creature to her.

Under a stack of folded linens, the uniforms

caught the sun from the window and sparkled. Marius swore.

Tahlia slid under his arm to look. "Oh. Those are…"

"Horrifying."

"Fantastic! But that's not what the other city guards were wearing."

"No, these are specifically for the parade guards, so we won't see them until we join the madness in an hour."

He pulled them out and handed her the smaller trousers, tunic, belt, and cloak. She took them with a grin that had no business here, then shouted, making him go for his blade again.

"A tomato hat!" She lifted a round sort of cap that had been stuffed between the trousers and tunic.

Could this get any worse? He doubted it.

Her hand darted toward him and she produced his hat, an even larger disaster of fabric as bright red as Ragewing's back. She hopped up and slammed the hat onto his head, then collapsed in a fit of snickering.

"You look amazing."

"Please stop talking and get dressed. The sooner we do this, the sooner I can have Ragewing burn this monstrous headgear into ash."

"But you said we have an hour before we need to blend in with the parade."

He only growled again and shook his leg to dislodge yet another furred tangle of chaos. He headed toward the hallway to disrobe, not wishing to do so in the company of the demons.

Smiling in that irresistible way she had, Tahlia joined him, and it was all he could do to keep from pulling her to him. It took every ounce of his rigorous training in self-discipline to refrain from running his palms up her smooth sides as she changed into the uniform's tunic. The bond between them hit him sometimes like this—incredibly powerful and completely out of nowhere. The feral side of him wished to cover her in his scent so the multitudes of people outside these walls would know she was his, but of course, that was a silly thought. They were humans, not Fae. But his blood didn't seem to give a shit.

"Oh, hells." He rushed toward her and pushed her against the wall as she smiled wide.

# CHAPTER 9
## MARIUS

"This is unexpected, Commander Marius."

Growling into her deliciously soft-scented neck, he pressed himself against her and savored her little moans of delight. His body rose to meet the challenge and he rubbed his length along her center. She gasped and lifted her hips. Pleasure coursed through Marius and his blood pounded in his ears.

Tahlia licked the tip of his ear, sending shivers of want down his neck and back. Gods, he wanted to ram himself into her with no regard for missions or crowns or humans with their heads up their arses. He longed to feel her warmth surrounding him in full.

"Another contact will be here shortly, won't he?" she asked in a breathy voice.

"Don't care," he muttered as he moved her carefully to the floor. There was a carpet lining the flat stone and it would keep the chill from her, not that he truly worried she might get cold with what activities he had in mind. "Be good, Tahlia. You want this, yes?"

He pulled away, suddenly worried he might have assumed too much. But she smiled saucily.

"Oh, yes, Marius. Yes, I do."

She helped him shuck off her Midhampton special guard trousers and his as well. Just the scent of her skin made his head swim...

His tongue licked its way down her bared stomach and she squirmed under him, her fingers digging into his scalp. Pinning her hips with his forearm, he brushed his mouth over her navel. He longed to take his time, but time wasn't something they had much of. At least one very tiny part of his mind was cognizant of that fact.

He met her gaze and she nodded, permitting him to continue. Rising up onto his elbow, he used his free hand to lift her leg. He drove into her and his body lit up with pleasure. The sensations roared through his blood. He kissed her hard and her mouth opened to him just as her body had. She felt like an afterlife he could never, ever deserve. Perfectly created for their joining.

"Perfect. You're perfect," he gasped out.

Her head fell back against the floor and she cried out, bucking her hips as she found her peak. He gripped her low around the hips, his hands squeezing her fine backside, and he thrust and thrust and thrust again until his climax claimed the last shred of his mind.

Falling gently onto her, feeling the movement of her blessed lungs and the beat of her darling heart, his pulse beat out one truth. "Mine. My mate. All mine."

"Aye, Commander Marius, and you are mine as well." She kissed the top of his head as he rested on her chest.

He hadn't realized he'd said the words aloud. A smile tugged at his lips and he held her close.

A fuzzy demon approached. It mewed directly into his face and marched onto his back. Marius growled and shifted his shoulder to dislodge the kitten, but the beastly thing held on with its foul claws. It curled up between his shoulder blades.

Tahlia dissolved in a fit of laughter. "The kitten..." She could barely speak and her laughter jostled his head. "Loves you."

A knock sounded, loud and so insistent that it had to have been going on for longer than they had noticed.

Removing the kitten from Marius's back, they hurried to clean up. In the water closet at the back of the house, they dressed while the knocking continued. Tahlia tucked Fara's letters under her tunic and into the waist of her trousers. They would be hidden, so he figured that was all right. If they were captured, their potions would fade and it wouldn't matter if the letters contained information that exposed Tahlia and Marius as Fae.

"I'm sorry I dragged you into lovemaking," Marius said.

"Don't apologize. I'll go again if you're up for it."

He froze in buttoning his trousers and eyed her smiling, beautiful face. "Do not tempt me, my mate. It's this city…" Moving on to fixing his tomato hat—*save me from this day, great Old Ones*—he continued his explanation. "With all these people around you, I feel the undeniable urge to mark you with my scent."

"Even though the humans won't detect it?"

"Yes. I know. I'm a beast."

She giggled and picked up the kitten who had befriended him. "A feral beast like this fellow?"

"Not *that* bad."

Her laugh eased his nerves and now that she smelled of him, of their union, his Fae blood cooled. Not completely, but some.

When Tahlia finally opened the door, the contact —a short human man with the same stupid costume they were wearing on his portly body—blinked at them.

He scowled at their faces, which were surely flushed. "I'm no Mist Knight," he whispered as he pushed past them and into the safe house's living room area, "but even I know *that* wasn't in the plan. Also, that hat is a lot on you, my dear man."

They followed him, Tahlia snickering. "It is." Her gaze traveled up to Marius's head.

Marius shut his eyes and begged all the powers of the world to make this day move more quickly from here on out.

The contact's gaze snagged on the pile of kittens that had dozed off in a square of sunlight near the hearth. He blew out a breath. Then he faced them again. "Your disguise spell is certainly working."

The way he said spell sounded akin to someone talking about a tragedy, but that was no surprise. Humans distrusted magic, and they believed the Fae were drenched in it. That was wrong, but perhaps they viewed some normal attributes as magical when indeed they were not. Marius wasn't sure.

"There is a change in plan," the contact said.

Marius crossed his arms. "Explain."

Tahlia bent to check the knife she had tucked into her boot. "What's happening?"

"Because of an incoming storm and the flooding that will likely be a problem in the Star Quarter of the city, King Durniad shortened the parade and will present himself, wearing the crown no doubt, in the morning. He will likely be at the fortress while you are attempting the heist. Once the tomato throwing begins, go to the fortress's southern entrance. Get in and get out. Use the name Edward Newlington, and once you're in, ask them if a storm is coming. If they're with us, they'll say, 'the sky and ocean are tricky.' Oh, and I meant to tell you that as hired guards, you'll fit in best if you participate in some of the foolish activities going on during the parade and so forth. Dance a dance if you're asked onto a stage. Have a drink, not five of them, mind you, but an ale or two will be expected on a festival day."

"Even from guards?" Tahlia asked.

"Yes. The guidelines for your behavior are up for debate. It'll all depend on which captain is bossing you about at the moment."

A spark of unpleasant heat sizzled under Marius's breastbone. "About what I would expect from humans who tolerate pirates," he said very quietly, unable to restrain himself.

The contact's gaze flicked to Marius's face, but he didn't say a word in retort. Perhaps he agreed.

"The crown is still hidden in the same place though, right? That hasn't changed?" Tahlia asked.

"As far as we know, the crown is still locked up somewhere under the fortress. You heard about the labyrinth and the potential traps, correct?" The contact removed a waterskin from his belt and sipped loudly. Sweat shone on his wide forehead.

Marius nodded as he and Tahlia packed their

clothing into a sack left for them on the table. "But no details. Do you know anything further?"

"No. Only that building out one of the traps resulted in the death of Durniad's right-hand man and a few people he viewed as less important."

"Details, please." Marius attached his dagger to the uniform's broad belt, using a loop with a long metal button.

Tahlia did the same and he appreciated the fact that she remembered to tuck an extra blade into her borrowed boot.

The contact replaced the waterskin at his belt, then mopped his brow with his loose linen sleeve. "Of course, yes. But we have little time. What I was told was that Durniad commanded his team to house something incredibly dangerous down there. His right-hand man told him it wasn't a good idea. When the trap or what-ever it is killed the man, Durniad claimed the advisor deserved the death for his disloyalty, then Durniad murdered those who had agreed with the advisor."

"Really nice guy, hmm?" Tahlia shook her head, her cheeks going pale.

"An absolute pig."

Tahlia nodded. "So no other clues other than generally very dangerous?"

Marius pressed his lips together. Going into this blind was not what he had in mind. He'd thought the contact would at least know something of Durniad's wild plan to house the crown.

"And no mention of the tools they used to set up the trap or any visiting experts?" Marius asked.

"Well, now that you mention it..." The contact bent at the waist as a sleepy-eyed monster with tabby stripes trotted up to his boot. He picked it up and stroked its back—he'd get fleas for sure. "Aside from the usual engineers employed in construction that close to the sea's edge, Durniad brought in a smithy."

"A blacksmith?" Tahlia asked.

The contact nodded as he returned the kitten to the floor. "One who is known to specialize in locks, doors, custom carts for hauling livestock. That sort of thing."

"Hmm." Marius tapped his chin. What was Durniad hoping to contain? The crown, obviously. But anything else? Would there be an elaborate trap that they could trigger upon entering the area where he had the crown hidden? Or perhaps a mechanism that made it so sharpened spearheads or blades set into the walls of the structure could be loosed from outside the building if they were seen entering?

"You know, it might not be a terrible idea to attempt to get information out of Durniad's brother, Jovanyth. He drinks too much, so Durniad basically ignores his existence," the contact said. "I tried to get him to talk to me when he was deep in his cups four days ago, but a friend of his spoiled my attempts."

"Where is this brother now?" Marius asked.

The contact waved his hand all around. "He's with everyone else. In the streets, celebrating."

"We will find him," Marius said.

"But—" the contact started, but Marius held up a hand.

"Information is the key to success. What tavern does he frequent?"

"The Siren's Grotto."

Tahlia raised her eyebrows, and the mischievous glint in her eyes brightened. "Sounds fun."

The contact snorted and Marius pondered what the sound meant to him. That the tavern wasn't fun? That Tahlia was being foolish? Marius felt his lip curl, but because of the Witch's potion, his Fae fang wouldn't show and properly threaten this fellow for insulting his mate.

Tahlia tugged on his guard uniform sleeve. "Eh, Commander, are you listening? You all right?"

Marius shook off his growing irritation with the contact and forced a smile. "You were saying..."

Swallowing, the contact dragged his gaze from Marius's fisted hand to look instead at Tahlia.

"Head up this road," he said, giving directions to the tavern. He went on with little details to look for and where to go, including a trip through the city's catacombs. "There is a torch or two sitting down there from our last use of the passage. A small bag should be beside them with flint and stone. It will only take a small spark to ignite the torch because it's doused in the same stuff Durniad uses in sea battles. Do not, and I repeat, do not get any of it on your skin. You might be powerful Fae beings, but I think it would still give you a pretty nasty wound to deal with in the middle of all this."

Marius nodded.

"The catacombs might be a little damp with the tide high," the human said. "Follow the crown symbol etched into the wall on each turn..." His directions continued, telling them how to get to the Siren's Grotto exactly. He told them to join the parade once they were finished with Jovanyth.

Marius crossed his arms. "Perfect. The tomato throwing begins at the sound of the explosions, yes?"

"The fireworks, yes. You'll hear some horns too."

"Do humans detonate fireworks often?" Tahlia asked. "Our king does, but the everyday person doesn't have access."

"No. Special events only. They're too expensive for most to purchase."

"Interesting. Thanks!"

The contact started to frown at Tahlia.

Marius stepped closer and stared down at the human. "Anything else?"

He coughed. "Ah, uh, no. That's it. But take this." Turning back toward the front door, he shoved a key into Marius's hand. "I nabbed it from one of the guards at the fortress's old gate. I'm not sure what it unlocks, but it can't hurt to have it."

"Thank you."

The contact left, and after a count of twenty, they did the same.

It was time to find a drunkard and squeeze him for information. If they missed their timing to get into the fortress, they would be caught. Their potion would wear off while in holding cells, no doubt, and then they would be at the mercy of Durniad.

Marius wasn't about to let anyone capture Tahlia even if he had to give his life to keep that from happening.

# CHAPTER 10

# TAHLIA

Between two three-story buildings, Tahlia trailed Marius down the set of stairs the safe house contact had told them about. They found one torch and the bag at the bottom of the stairs.

"Keep watch behind us," Marius ordered as he worked to light the torch.

Watery light from the street level filtered down to Tahlia and the noise of the crowd bounced off the carved pale stones. Wind from farther into the catacombs blew lightly like the breath of a ghost. Tahlia shivered.

Marius held the fiery torch up. "All right. I will go first. Every ten steps or so, be sure to look back to check for anyone creeping up behind."

"Will do, Commander."

The plain stone walls gave way to stacks of elaborately organized skulls, femurs, and ribcages. Some skeletons were arranged to appear like they were walking along the wall. Others lay in carved-out alcoves. A massive triangle of skulls marked an archway. The right-side passage was marked with the little carved crown that the safe house contact had mentioned. They turned in that direction and more bones greeted them.

"This is wild," Tahlia said, eyeing it all by the light of the flickering torch Marius carried.

Marius made his thinking noise.

"Their bones look like ours," she said, pondering humans in general.

"But they aren't like ours at all. Our bone density is three times theirs."

"How do you know that?"

"Albus," Marius said.

"When did he teach you?" she asked.

"For a while, as a youth, I thought perhaps I could learn some Healer skills for the battlefield. Beyond basic bandaging and how to stop bleeding."

"Why did you stop training?"

"To be honest, it bored me."

Tahlia huffed a laugh. "I can imagine you taking notes from Albus and longingly watching dragons take off outside the window."

"That is an accurate imagining."

"I never could sit still for learning either," Tahlia said.

They came to a room of sorts with a high, domed ceiling and began searching for the crown carving. Five corridors branched off from the room. A particularly large display of femurs created the shape of a lion that stretched from one side of the ceiling to the other. Tahlia went to the first corridor on the right to look for the crown.

"Nothing here."

Marius was across the room, smoothing his hand over the archway on the middle corridor. "I haven't found one yet either."

Tahlia went to the second corridor's entrance. Most of the passageways were stone, but this one had a wooden lintel. Old paint showed the faded remains of a river and three large structures set around its snakelike form. Beneath the right side, a crown had been painted in black.

"Do you think this counts? It's not carved, but it's definitely a crown."

Marius joined her and studied the painted image. "Since we can't find another, I think we should try it."

They continued onward, the sound of the city above silenced by the depth of the catacombs.

Marius stopped and Tahlia ran into his back.

"What is it?" she whispered, her heart hammering.

"Footsteps."

Tahlia drew her dagger and held her breath to listen. His ears were so much better than hers. It was frustrating.

"They're coming. Two males. Humans."

The sound of whispering and quick boot steps echoed through the dimness. Two men in muddied clothing rounded the corner, faces going slack with shock.

One with a red beard recovered first. A sly grin slithered over his mouth. "Well, well. A couple of guards keeping watch on the old bones." He rubbed his hands together. "Ripe for the picking, seems like to me." He jerked his chin in the direction of Marius's tomato hat.

"I assure you that you do not want to bother us," Marius said.

The fool was too dumb to be scared of that tone and he lunged for Marius. His friend, a man with a tiny knife and only one tooth at the front of his mouth, went for Tahlia.

Marius slammed into Red Beard, knocking the man into the wall. He exhaled in a gust of curses and raised a fist to strike.

Tahlia lifted her arms and dove into Toothy's attack—one forearm at his neck and the other hitting his arm. Her left hand slid down that arm until she had his wrist held firmly with his sad, wee knife locked away from her body. She looped the hand at his neck around the back of his skull and bent him low. She kneed him in the nose. He shrieked, dropped the knife, and fell against the far wall.

Marius had his assailant on the ground, his foot on the man's chest. Marius's eyes burned with unspent fury. "Did he injure you?" he asked Tahlia.

She grabbed the tiny fallen knife, then grabbed her attacker and threw him down beside his friend. "Nope. I'm fine. Should we tie them up?"

"Yes. We can report them to our superior once we have finished canvassing the catacombs."

Ah, right. He was pretending to be a city guard. Tahlia frowned, watching how his eyes burned as he looked at them. Yes, they were terrible people, but that rage... seemed over the top. Maybe it was because she was his mate. Males did become rather insane with protectiveness once fully married and mated. Or was it because they were humans and they dared to attack them? And human pirates *had* killed his sister. He did seem to hate humans with a special level of passion.

# CHAPTER 11

# TAHLIA

Three different songs wailed through the streets of Midhampton. Locals and visitors alike danced the same quick-step jig, drank ale from pale crockery cups, and laughed together.

"It's marvelous," Tahlia said, doing her best to keep moving. Marius kept gently urging her forward with a hand to the small of her back.

"It's chaos."

"What would you rather be doing right now? Sitting in your chair at Dragon Tail Peak with one of your saucy novels?"

He growled over her shoulder. She glanced up at his handsome, scarred face and grinned.

"How do you know about my reading choices?"

"I'm your mate. You think you're sneaky, putting

that military history book on top of your romances, but I'm not fooled."

"Well, I'll thank you not to mention my preferences regarding books in public."

"Nobody here knows us."

His breath was suddenly at her ear. "Hush, female, or I shall have to tie you up when we get home and punish you for disrespecting your commander."

"Oooh, promise?"

A chuckle rumbled in his chest, vibrating into her back as they took the third right.

The Siren's Grotto sign swung in the sea breeze.

"There!" Tahlia pointed.

Marius trailed her through the tavern's round oaken door. "Remember, they'll call us dogs. That's the term for hired guards."

Tahlia nodded. "Adorable."

Pipe smoke clouded the air inside and the voices of at least twenty patrons echoed off the low ceiling.

A hand clamped down on Tahlia's forearm. She whipped around, her hand on the hilt of her dagger. Marius came up behind the man who'd grabbed her and had set a blade beside his throat in a movement that blurred with speed. He moved so incredibly fast. And he was going to blow their cover. Unless of course, everyone here was too sloshed to notice.

The man let go of Tahlia and held up his hands. "Easy, dogs. I was only going to offer you a drink for your services today." His smile was missing a tooth, but that was probably poor hygiene, not from fighting. He was a lump of a fellow.

Marius lowered his weapon and nodded for Tahlia to relax.

"Sorry," Tahlia said, taking on a casual tone. "We've had some real idiots to deal with already today, so we're on edge."

The man chuckled and waved them to the barkeep's counter. "I can imagine." He faced the keep and handed over a few coins. "Three of your best, please."

The ale was bitter but very cold. Tahlia forced herself not to gulp it down. She needed her wits about her. Marius was only pretending to drink. She'd seen him fake it before; he tended to furrow his brow when he was actually drinking.

Knowing Marius might murder her for the recklessness but also certain they had no time to waste, Tahlia went ahead and asked a probing question. "I bet King Durniad has called in every last soul down to his own brother to watch these wild crowds."

Marius's mouth tightened to a line, but he kept his gaze on the man and pretended to sip his ale.

The man grinned and glanced toward a weasel-eyed man at a small, square table near the back wall. Had to be the brother, Jovanyth. Marius and Tahlia exchanged a look.

"Well, he isn't that desperate, I don't think," the man said. "Your accent is unusual. Where do you two hail from?"

Marius pretended to be very thirsty while Tahlia answered with their cover story. "We're cousins. Our parents were traveling merchants, so we picked up a little of everything along the way."

Shoulders relaxing, the man appeared to swallow her lie. "Ah, so that's why you sound like a Veiler."

Veiler? Perhaps that was what they called folk who lived close to the Veil.

"Oh, look," Marius said to Tahlia, his gaze going to a terrible painting at the back of the tavern. "The use of lighting in that piece is very well done."

Tahlia stifled a snort of laughter. She elbowed the man. "My cousin has a passion for the arts."

The man frowned, then shrugged. "I never thought a hired dog would care a whit for paintings…" His gaze twisted into a look stuffed with suspicion.

A woman in a very tight and revealing corset bumped into him and giggled. The man turned to face her fully and seemed to forget about Tahlia and Marius, which was a stroke of good luck. Phew.

Marius waved Tahlia toward the painting.

"Now, what do you love so much about this one, dear cousin?" she said loudly as they approached Jovanyth's table. "And how did you lie about the lighting?" she whispered, laughing.

"I closed my eyes and imagined a painting at the castle."

"Good one."

"It's not my first mission, Lady Tahlia," he whispered under the din of the tavern.

Tahlia accidentally bumped into Jovanyth. "I wonder who the artist is?"

Durniad's brother grunted and glared at Tahlia with swollen eyes. "Eh, watch your big arse, dog."

Marius's nostrils flared and he bared his teeth. He was going to blow this thing up.

CHAPTER 12

# TAHLIA

Sweating, Tahlia touched his arm. He shut his eyes and his chest moved in a deep breath.

Tahlia faced the king's brother and smiled. "Here, take my ale in apologies, my lord."

"I'm no lord, but I'll take it just the same." He grinned at her, snatched the ale, and then drank it down in three swallows.

She clapped and laughed like it was the greatest feat she'd ever witnessed. Marius, who was pretending to study the painting, looked like he was about to burst from trying not to roll his eyes or beat the man to death. Perhaps both.

"I have always wanted to meet the most powerful man in Midhampton."

"That's my brother," Jovanyth said, winking, "not me, lass."

"Ah, but he would do whatever you asked, I'm guessing, and that's the best kind of power."

Marius had told her that humans cared for control above all else, and she really hoped that was true for at least this one fellow. If he was, instead, say, more focused on loyalty, this little conversation she was attempting would rankle the king's brother instead of opening him up.

Jovanyth set his mug down and pointed at her. "You are a smart one, aren't you?" His words knocked together like untied urns in the back of a mule cart. "Why don't you sit here and chat with me for a while? Or will your man there get his feathers ruffled?"

She dismissed Marius with the wave of her fingers and sat in the chair opposite the king's brother. "My cousin is perpetually ruffled, so don't even worry about that."

The anger rolling off Marius was almost palpable, but he stayed in character and began to discuss the upcoming tomato throwing with a man and a woman wearing thick aprons stained with dyes.

Tahlia leaned over the table and began to whisper to Jovanyth. "So I heard your brother has a big surprise for the end of the festivities."

A flicker of distrust shaded the drunk man's eyes, but he shook his head and laughed, the sound bouncing off the low ceiling. He rifled through a pack strung across his chair and removed a pipe.

"Where did you hear this, pretty one?"

She smacked Marius's hip, and when he turned, she stole his ale. Marius allowed it and he quickly went back to his conversation with the couple. Tahlia sipped the ale, then slowly licked a drop off her top lip. Jovanyth watched her movements like a lion preparing to pounce.

*Don't even try it, pal. Marius will eviscerate you and that will ruin everyone's day.*

"I don't remember where I heard it." She tipped her mug back and took a good gulp. When she set it back on the table, he was studying her a bit too closely. "Oh, yes, I do." She laughed, loud and sure as he had. As if she hadn't a care in the world. "It was from that arse-head, Domi. He's always getting his prick into private conversations."

A smile cracked Jovanyth's frowning face. "Liked by the noble ladies, your friend?"

"Yes. He's, um, how should I say this?"

"Blessedly endowed."

Not actually entertained, she slapped the table and feigned being lost in hilarity. He joined in and called for a server to bring them another round.

Tahlia met Marius's gaze for a second. His eyes questioned her, and she gave a barely perceptible nod. Yes, she was all right. It was working.

"My arrogant-as-the-sun brother has something

dangerous, I'm sure. It'll be all well for him and shit for the rest of us, as usual."

"Can't you benefit being his sibling?"

"No." He took the ales from the server and handed her one. His was half gone by the time he set the mug back down. A belch rumbled from him and Tahlia forced her features to remain in a vaguely happy position. "The bastard set up a whole series of traps around whatever it is." Leaning forward, he whispered, "Even a siren. There's a damned siren down there under the fortress. Can you believe it?"

Tahlia's body froze. No. It couldn't be. "I thought..." Her mouth didn't want to work and it had zero to do with the ale.

"That they weren't real? Yeah." He barked a laugh. "I didn't think they were either until his arse returned from the north with one. She's horrifying, and that's saying a lot considering she has the body of a goddess and the face of a dream."

"She can kill with a song?"

"Saw it myself," he whispered, leaning too far to the right. He was about to fall out of his chair, the fool.

"Wait. What did you say?"

"I saw her use her song myself."

"You did?"

"Aye. One of my brother's dear engineers lunged to grab her and before anyone realized her muzzle had slipped, she stopped his heart with three little notes."

Goosebumps ran down Tahlia's arms and she shivered.

"Exactly," he said, nodding toward her. "That was my reaction too. See, she can direct the kill and can only take one soul at a time. The man was doomed just because she exudes desire and the poor man couldn't hold himself back. Could have been me. Easy." He upturned his mug and banged the bottom as if more ale might come out if he only tried harder.

A siren. They had to face a siren to get the crown.

"Old Durny boy tried to cage her and that went really well, too." Jovanyth chuckled and shook his head. "Had to bargain with her. You see, our family has a history with the sirens…" He set an elbow on the table and leaned his chin into his hand.

Was he passing out? Right here, right now?

Marius made his way over and jerked his head toward the door. "We have to get going."

Jovanyth lifted his hand, his ale-glazed eyes half open. "Enjoy the madness and stay out of my brother's path if you know what's good for you."

Tahlia swallowed, murmured a thanks, and left quickly. Marius was right behind her when they emerged back into the sunshine. Dark clouds rolled in the distance, and thunder rumbled over the sound of the crowd.

"Don't talk now," Marius said as they forced their way through the masses toward the line of guards dressed as they were. "We'll walk the outer edge of the crowd until the parade starts, then branch off."

Ten tidy rows of pipers, flag bearers, and folk with small drums lined up. Guards dressed as Tahlia and Marius were—in the ornate clothing and ridiculous hat—created a boundary between the crowds and the musicians. People wearing fine gowns filed in behind the musicians. Perhaps the local nobility or simply the wealthy of the city? Durniad would be among them.

Tahlia tugged at Marius's sleeve. "Did you hear what he told me? Any of it?"

"Not now."

They passed three other guards.

"Fall in line," one of the other guards barked at them, making Tahlia's stomach clench with worry. His bushy eyebrows furrowed as he studied them. "You two smell like an alehouse."

Tahlia grinned and shrugged. "You can't tell me my cousin and I are the only two sneaking a drink today."

Master Eyebrows scowled, but the guard at his side elbowed him.

"Lay off, Sergee. Everything's fine."

"All right, but I'm watching you."

Marius nodded at Eyebrows. That man had no idea that he was trying to intimidate the Shadow of the Shrouded Mountains, a Fae warrior who had taken down countless pirates, enemy armies, and more. It was laughable that the fellow thought he was in a position of power. Granted, he could sound an alarm before Marius or Tahlia had the chance to dispatch him to the afterlife, and this was meant to be a quiet mission...

Tahlia marched obediently between Marius and Eyebrows, who snarled at a woman who had let her child run into the street.

The music began and all Tahlia could think about was Jovanyth's mention of the siren's song. Sure, one could block one's ears, but many stories claimed sirens had the ability to send their power into your very bones. No rolls of cloth stuffed in the ears would stop such a magic.

Tahlia recalled a little storybook she'd seen in the market once when she was maybe ten or eleven years old. The story had included some truly dismal poems, including one about a siren. The whole thing had been penned in blue ink and it stood out in her mind's eye like she'd seen it yesterday.

She sings, she lures,
You listen, you lunge,
Into the cold blue-black, you go,
She'll drag you low, low, low,
Into the sea's dark arms you flow,
Pulled to pieces,
Knocked utterly senseless,
A song, a touch, and you're a memory forgotten.

She snorted at herself, darkly amused. *Great work remembering that horror but missing Fara's birthday last year.* Oh, gods, how Fara would be sounding the alarm if she knew that a siren was involved in this venture to Midhampton.

"Almost there," Marius whispered.

"What?" Eyebrows leaned forward to frown at Marius across from Tahlia.

A tomato soared from the crowd to the left and splashed onto a piper's head.

"Eh! Not time yet!" the piper shouted, his complaint backed up by several others calling out and shaking their fists.

"All these people have tomatoes already," Tahlia said, more to herself than anyone.

"Yes," Eyebrows said gruffly. "Of course they do. Have you never been to the Tomatina Festival?"

"Not to the one here in Midhampton."

"There are no others."

"No, there's another one. In, umm, in Deigs."

The guard who'd elbowed Eyebrows made a *huh* sound. "Really?"

Another tomato flew overhead. A shout followed. Two more tomatoes dashed across the gathered humans. One smashed into a woman who laughed and wiped her face. The other hit a drummer. The drummer threw a punch at a man to his right, who hit him back.

"Get up there and get them marching again," Eyebrows ordered Marius.

Marius nodded and started off with a glance in Tahlia's direction. Without waiting for a command from the actual guards, she followed Marius.

A little girl with bright blue eyes slipped from her father's watch and ran into the parade, dashing behind Tahlia. Tahlia whirled and snagged the girl's arm. She eased her away from the pipers and the men Marius was barking at, then deposited her into her father's arms.

"Thank you, guard."

"Of course," Tahlia said.

She wanted to study the human's face, looking for differences between human facial features and Fae's, but there was no time. She couldn't lose Marius. Whipping around, she took off to find her spot behind him again.

"How did breaking the fight up go?"

"I think I bruised an arm. Accidentally, of course."

Tahlia grimaced. "It's not easy to be careful, I'm sure." He was easily three times as strong as a human male.

The music continued, and the marching carried on until the parade had snaked its way through the streets. They kept in line as much as they could until their fellow guards began to pass flasks and skins of various blends of alcohol to one another. Then order started to fall apart pretty quickly.

They came to a wooden stage, one of several they'd seen throughout the city streets.

"You two, up, up, now," Eyebrows demanded.

"Why isn't he drunk yet?" Tahlia whispered as he shoved them toward the stage.

"Because it's a mission and nothing is ever easy."

Tahlia grinned wryly and walked up the three steps to the stage, where a woman in a long red gown embroidered in tomatoes was finishing up a song about sailors, storms, and a dance that had apparently stopped a flood.

"And here they are!" the woman shouted, gesturing to Tahlia and Marius.

Marius froze, his glare admirable considering the hat currently residing on his head.

The woman grinned. "Ah, I see that he is the storm."

The crowd's noise coalesced into a great cheer for Marius.

Tahlia elbowed him. "See? I'm not the only one who thinks you are rather delightfully stormy. Also, I think we need to drop the cousins cover and play this up as a couple."

Marius turned his scowl on her and she giggled.

The woman clapped her hands three times and the

crowd quieted somewhat. They came closer to the stage, holding baskets of tomatoes.

"The lass must be our dancer, then!" the woman said.

Another cheer went up, and Tahlia bowed dramatically, glad her perfectly ridiculous hat had a chin strap. She wouldn't have wanted to lose it.

She was having the time of her life.

"Let's see what you can do, Storm!" the woman ordered.

Marius stood there, as calm and deadly as he ever was. The mass of people booed him and waved fists.

"The tomatoes will come next if you don't get to work," Tahlia said to him out of the corner of her mouth.

"This is madness. We need to get back to the street and get to the goal."

"I doubt this group here is going to let us off the hook." Tahlia jerked her chin at the people in the front row. Their faces were flushed with sun and ale both, and their eyes were just crazy enough to worry about. "Stomp around and growl. You're good at this. It's just another day at the job for you, love."

He growled all right and it didn't sound human at all. A hush began to sweep through the folks gathered close. She had to do something. Now.

She began skipping around Marius. "What a lovely day at the coastline," she sang, making notes up as she went. A few people laughed and one shouted something about Tahlia's arse. She only sang louder. "A lovely, lovely morn!" Gods, her voice was a tragedy, but she had to give it all she had. "I can't imagine there ever being a terrible moment of weather with the sky like this!" She tapped the top of his head, then leaned up and kissed the end of his nose.

The crowd burst into cheers and warnings of the storm to come, even as the actual sky overhead rumbled with real thunder.

"Come on, now." She poked his ribs on her next go round.

Marius, his tunic tight across his broad chest and his eyes unblinking, stomped his foot and the whole stage quaked. He lifted his head and let out a weak growl. Good. He'd realized his last one was far too feral to be a sound a human male would make.

"Ooooh!" the woman cooed and clapped, urging the crowd to make more noise for the storm.

Marius stomped again, then lifted his other foot and did a little double stomp.

"Oh, that is scary," Tahlia said to the gathering, clasping her hands at her chin dramatically.

"Flood the town!" the woman demanded. Then she leaned close to Marius. "Lift her over your shoulder, man. You should know the traditions. Where are they getting guards these days?"

She sounded beyond exhausted with them, and

Tahlia couldn't help but chuckle. Marius rolled his eyes, then lifted Tahlia onto his shoulder.

"Spin her 'round!"

"Toss her down!"

It was a chant that all the people took up. Tahlia laughed as Marius did as commanded. He pinched her leg lightly and grumbled, "You are not allowed to find this entertaining."

"Sure, Master Guard. Sure."

She laughed harder as he cradled her, tossed her into the air a bit, then caught her, all to the happy cheers of the crowd.

"Now, dance him into submission!" the people cried out.

The woman clapped her hands over her head in a steady rhythm that the city folk took up quickly. It became a deafening drum of palms as Marius set her down. She pretended to lift a make-believe dress and danced about Marius with steps that matched the clapping. The rhythm sped up, faster and faster, until Tahlia was out of breath and nearly falling into Marius. He caught her, and if she hadn't seen it herself, she would never have believed it, but Marius actually grinned. His eyes danced as surely as she had as he dipped her low and kissed her fully to the excited cries of the crowd.

# CHAPTER 13

# MARIUS

Tahlia kissed him back, then smiled as he helped her off the stage.

He shook his head as they made their way back to Eyebrows. "Torturous nonsense."

"Interesting way to say *fun*," Tahlia whispered.

"Well done, you two," the guard captain with the generous eyebrows said. "Now, fill in the gaps as the parade comes to a close."

Perfect. Now they had the freedom to move about without eliciting too much unwanted attention.

"Watch for overly aggressive participants when the throwing begins," the captain added.

"Aye," Marius said, feigning obedience. It wasn't a lie to simply agree, but his heart knew they wouldn't be doing as ordered so the word still tasted like deceit

—a sharp bitterness at the back of his tongue and a branching pain through his temples.

He led Tahlia through the crowd, past several docks. The sea beyond the bay was gray and it chewed at the rocky crescent that protected the docked boats and anchored ships. Following his mental map of the city, he hurried Tahlia along until they were back on the main south road, right in front of the fortress. The crowd was shoulder to shoulder, and their pace slowed to a near crawl.

The sky cracked, and it wasn't lightning. Fire-blooms, fireworks, some called them. Sparks like dragon fire bloomed over the city in an array of gold, black, blue, and red. The people crowed and howled like forest creatures and the madness began.

Tomatoes. Everywhere.

Tahlia snagged a tomato from the air and tossed the half-squished thing at a random human.

"Guard," Marius growled at Tahlia, a fierce protectiveness crashing through his Fae blood. Humans could twist into monsters at a moment's notice.

The human female Tahlia had hit with the tomato turned and laughed, lugging one back at Tahlia. Fine. She seemed so happy to be involved in the chaos, but truly, they didn't have time for this. They needed to get into the fortress before the two humans who'd agreed to work with them were traded out for the new shift.

But Tahlia's laugh and her dancing eyes made it impossible for him to pull her along or complain. Though she was covered in red juice and pieces of tomato, she was so damn beautiful. He did miss seeing her Fae fangs though since they were cloaked by the Witch's potion.

With a yelp, she slipped. He shot his arm out without thinking, and he caught her, then pulled her close. Her damp uniform did little to hide her blessed curves.

"Careful, little salty. You might tempt me to ignore all of humankind just to drag you into an alcove and have my way with you."

"I wish you were truly tempted!" She laughed into his chest, then looked up at him with those lovely eyes of hers.

Even though the glamour cloaked her eyes, their true beauty shone through nonetheless.

She continued. "But I know you're dying for me to stop having fun and get back to the job."

Normally, he would never be so tempted to take his time during a mission. "I'm torn, honestly. It's the bond."

She reached up and kissed him hard, and he stepped back, chuckling and surprised. A human male careened into them. Marius slid, grabbed at the corner of a building, but fell to his arse anyway. Tahlia reached for him and landed sideways on top of his chest. Both their stupid hats were gone, thank the gods. She laughed again, and her body moved against his, scattering his thoughts. The sun broke through the churning storm clouds for a moment. The light behind her head made her look like a goddess. He kissed her, allowing his wilder side to satiate itself somewhat. He ran his fingers through her sticky hair.

"You taste like dinner," she whispered against his tomato-drenched mouth.

Another chuckle tripped from his lips as they helped one another up all while getting pummeled with yet more tomatoes. A man with a dramatic beard and mustache reached out his hands to aid them. Marius shook his head, but Tahlia took one hand and shook it.

She should have been more wary around humans.

"This is so fun. I love your town," she said to the man.

"Glad you could make it!" The fellow nodded, then went back to participating in the melee.

Marius paused in tossing tomatoes to watch Tahlia as she stared at the crowd. Something dark churned inside him. Why did he feel terrible about her enjoying herself?

Well, firstly, because they were on a mission. That made good sense. Also, this frivolity was probably ruining their schedule. What else though? She appeared to truly appreciate the company of humans.

She didn't seem fazed by the fact that they were generally weak-willed, and disloyal, and evil.

Did she possibly prefer human company?

He pulled at the neck of his tunic and tried to step away from the humans up against his right side.

Would Tahlia long for this feeling after they left this place?

Would he ever be enough for her?

Surely, she didn't prefer humans. He shook his head to clear it, then waved a hand to get her moving.

She thrust two more tomatoes into the crowd, her face lit with joy, then she faced him, smiled, and hurried to his side.

"Do we need to search this soup to find our hats?" she asked, eyeing the mash of tomatoes under the feet of everyone around them.

"If you do nothing else for me for eternity, please forget about the hats."

Snickering, she started toward the fortress with him at her side.

This was strange. He was feeling so... He wasn't sure. So wrong? Ill?

Normally, her smile broke apart the clouds that tended to gather around his heart, but that dark feeling didn't fade under her bright attention this time. Instead, it grew stronger. He gritted his teeth as they wound their way to the fortress's side entrance. He had to stop feeling like this. It was foolish. She loved him and he knew that. They were mated. Bonded as surely as they were to their dragons.

The fortress loomed high above the riotous mass of people. Its walls were made of sandy-hued stone, and crenelations along the top housed archers. The archers stood quietly, watching without their bows ready. The report that King Lysanael had given Marius and Tahlia hadn't mentioned archers. This was another barrier they would have to get through.

The side door was unmarked—a simple slender rectangle of hardwood. He knocked and a small window at the top of the door slid open.

"Name?"

"Edward Newlington."

Tahlia was biting her lip, her eyes laughing at the name. Marius gave her a good glare so she'd remember they were on duty.

The small window shut with a thud.

Was it not one of their inside contacts at the door? Were they too late for the two they were meant to meet here? Marius looked up to see an archer staring down at them.

Marius breathed in and out slowly. Tahlia touched his arm as if she wanted to ask a question. But as he looked at her, the whole door swung open, and two people grabbed them and dragged them inside.

He had both humans by the throat against the small entryway's wall before a word could be uttered.

"Is there a storm coming?" he asked, using the code question.

The human squirming under his left hand tried to speak. Tahlia tapped Marius's hand.

"Might want to let him talk. Just a suggestion."

Marius nodded and loosened his hold. Slightly.

The human coughed and her freckled forehead wrinkled. "The sky and ocean are tricky."

It was the right code response. Marius released the two women.

The one on the left rubbed at her throat with a freckled hand and glared. "He's here early. Follow Maude to our room below. You'll have to stay the night and wait until he's gone," she whispered.

The second guard—a female with dark eyes like Tahlia's and very fair skin—grimaced even as she studied Marius and Tahlia with uncloaked curiosity.

"Our disguises are in place for your eyes still, yes?" Marius asked.

The two nodded.

Tahlia stepped closer, her gaze on the empty entryway and a set of doors beyond, doors that led into the fortress's central hall.

"Durniad is here?" Tahlia asked in a whisper.

"Aye. And he is in a state," the dark-eyed, fair-skinned guard said. "Stay on my heels. Walk quickly. He's feasting in his upper rooms at the moment, so we should be all right to scurry across the hall and down the back steps."

"Why can't we access the trove tonight if he is all the way up there?" Marius asked.

"Because he will want to show off his labyrinth to his cronies after he eats his weight in pastries."

Tahlia lifted her eyebrows. He knew that look— she was dreaming of pastries instead of thinking of labyrinths. He almost smiled even though they were definitely off their schedule now.

"Our disguises will fail before we can escape the city if we wait to breach the trove."

"I know. The safe house contact sent a raven to your king and queen with a request for aid."

A headache squeezed Marius's temples with alarming ferocity. He rubbed his forehead with his fingers. That should not have been necessary.

"Do you know anything about a siren?" Marius asked.

The guard looked appropriately horrified. "I don't. They kept us from the traps and didn't permit anyone to talk about them or ask questions. Ovain, one of the other guards, asked about them and no one has seen him since."

Marius and Tahlia exchanged a look.

Tahlia rubbed her tomato-coated hands together. "So it's a smash-and-grab and run-for-your-life mission now, hmm?"

"Perhaps we can go in as soon as Durniad and his friends depart late tonight," Marius suggested.

The freckled guard shrugged. "You can try, but he parties until the early hours of the morning when he's riled up like this." A shudder shook her frame and she muttered what sounded like a prayer.

"I don't want to know what a fellow like him thinks is fun," Tahlia said, frowning.

"No, you do not," Marius said. He wanted to say something about humans' general penchant for gore and power, but he didn't want to upset the guards with so much riding on their performance tonight.

"I'll get you to our room," the fair guard said, "and then I'll get you to the trove before dawn."

"Agreed," Marius said.

The guard went to the doors beyond and pushed one open. The group of three rushed through the entrance. Marius and Tahlia's clothing dripped tomato as they went.

"What about this mess?" Tahlia whispered over her shoulder at Marius.

There weren't any other guards present in the hall —only a row of painted portraits along the front of the room and an empty table stacked with small wooden boxes that were set at each place like gifts to those who would eat here later.

"I'll tidy up as soon as you're locked in," the guard said. She turned the corner and ushered them down a dark set of stairs. The scent of the sea touched Marius's nose.

"What is in those boxes?" Marius asked.

"They're tiny wooden contraptions. I'm not sure what they are," the guard said. "I only heard they were symbolic presents for visitors who would arrive tomorrow before the presentation of the crown. Something about showing off new additions. I don't know what that means, honestly." She moved onward.

Marius frowned, then nodded at Tahlia to catch up with the guard.

At the base of the stairs, the guard veered right, and they snaked their way down to a row of doors.

"The second one is mine," the guard said. "It's open. Locks from the inside. Stay there until we come for you. No matter what you hear. I stashed some corncakes in the dresser if you're hungry."

"What do you mean no matter what we hear?" Tahlia asked.

"I have to go." The guard left without a backward glance.

Tahlia went ahead of Marius and opened the door to a small chamber. Marius quickly surveyed the space, checking for watch holes that could have been carved into the walls and if any runes had been etched into the simple bed, dresser, or desk.

"All clear." His heart was beating too quickly. Having his mate here was undeniably distracting—he could no longer fool himself that it wasn't—and though he knew she was quick, smart, and quite capable, he couldn't help wishing she was back at Dragon Tail Peak, in the safety of the castle walls.

"Are we supposed to have a change of clothes in here? I can't remember," Tahlia asked.

Marius flipped the quilt on the bed back to reveal two stacks of dark clothing. He handed one to Tahlia. "You seem to really enjoy this tomatina nonsense," he said, trying for a casual tone even though the words meant more. What exactly, he wasn't yet certain.

# CHAPTER 14

# TAHLIA

Tahlia studied Marius's face as she set the dark clothing on the end of the bed. She undid her belt, set it on the ground, then removed Fara's letters from where she'd stashed them—tucked neatly into her trousers. She set the letters on the bedside table near a bowl of water, a candle and flint set, and a stack of clean cloths.

When she glanced back, Marius wasn't looking her way. Something was off. His shoulders were tense and pulled up toward his ears like he was bracing for a strike for which he had no defense.

"It's throwing vegetables, listening to music, acting like fools, and drinking ale. What's not to love?"

"Humans. And it's a fruit, not a vegetable."

Tahlia's heart cinched. "Marius, look at me."

"If you need help with washing your hair, I'm happy to—"

She tugged at his arm and finally he met her gaze. "Of course I'm enjoying this festival."

"You are enjoying being around humans."

"So? I'm half-human. What do you expect?"

His throat moved in a swallow and he held her gaze. "Full humans are terrible creatures."

Her chest caved, and she set a hand on his tomato-stained tunic. "Marius..."

"I mean," he said, looking away, "generally. Not all of them."

"You still believe that nonsense after choosing a mate with their blood? After working with a queen who is human?"

His lip curled. He turned away, running a hand over the back of his neck. He had tomato bits in his hair that she longed to comb away.

"Tahlia, I, no, I don't think I do believe humans are worse than Fae. Not anymore."

She sagged, leaning her hands on her knees. "That's basically the opposite of what you just said."

She expected him to whirl around and smile, to kiss her and apologize. But instead, he focused on the wall, his silence deafening.

"Marius, what is it?" He had to be thinking of his sister and how human pirates were the ones to end her life. But those humans were bad ones. There were horrible Fae too. He knew that, but his demeanor said he was having a hard time feeling the truth of it.

"I don't know," he replied quietly. "I truly don't know. Seeing you here, among these people, it makes me angry. Maybe I am worried I won't be enough for you. That you might want to leave the Fae realm someday and live among humans. They're more relaxed than us. I know that now."

"They are a blast, honestly. Do you think they'd accept a dragon rider and her scary Seabreak?"

He glanced at her, worry pinching his gaze. Maybe her silliness had been a bad move for this intense moment.

She held up her hands. "I'm joking. Marius, I adore you. I would never, ever leave you. Just because these idiots south of the Veil know how to party doesn't mean I'm planning to make a life here. I love our life at home. I hope you know I'm not that shallow." How could he ever think she would leave?

His head fell back, and he shut his eyes as he exhaled. He opened his eyes and looked at her, then he pulled her into his arms.

She pressed her lips into the hollow at the base of his throat. "You are my home, Marius. Wherever you are, that's where I am happiest."

His mouth was warm on the top of her damp hair. He kissed the crown of her head and gently held her close, his thumb stroking the bottom of her ear and the soft spot beside her jaw. Beneath the tomatoes, he smelled like he always did. And it was wonderful. Familiar and exciting, both.

"I adore you. You are well aware of that," he said quietly. "Perhaps I'm only being overprotective. This is a messy mission. The dangers continue to multiply."

"That makes sense." She pulled back a bit. His eyes had softened and he was almost smiling, the right side of his full lips tugged up a fraction of an inch. "Are we all right now? Can we get out of these terrible clothes and have a bit of merriment while we wait on her?"

She went to the bedside table, took up one of the cloths, and dipped it into the water.

"Merriment?" Marius's tone was lighter now.

Tahlia relaxed. She returned to Marius's side to clean his face. He sighed at her ministrations as she tidied his proud nose and brow, his cheekbones and jawline. She rewet the cloth and wiped down his neck, powerful forearms, and his fingers.

When she finished, he took up a new cloth and did the same for her. He found a wide comb and used it to wet and detangle her hair before tending to his own. She shucked off her boots and stockings. Her tunic's tie was knotted at the back of her neck, and she couldn't get the thing worked loose.

"Here." Marius breathed against the nape of her neck, and warmth traveled over her skin like his breath was sunlight. "Allow me, Lady of the Skies."

His deft fingers undid the knot with no trouble. He smoothed the tunic over her shoulder and peeled it from her, allowing her to step out. He worked the rest of her clothing off, then she took a turn to undress him, savoring the process. The corded muscle in his forearms and stomach. The narrow path between his hipbones. The male scent of him, the warmth of his inner thighs. His delightfully enormous cock. The smoldering look in his stormy eyes. The way his fingers twitched as if he was dying to grab her and do wonderfully naughty things to her.

He brought her to him and kissed her sweetly, his hands cradling her face. "Would my lady order me to my knees or does she have other merriment in mind?"

Rubbing himself slowly against her core, he drew a moan from her. Heat shot through her blood. He licked her breast and toyed with her nipple, sending shivers down her trembling thighs. She couldn't summon a single word. He dropped down and held her arse as she stood before him. His tongue explored her, and pleasure coursed up her center. Her breath came in only gasps now as he drove her mad with flicks, swirls, and thrusts with his mouth and fingers. He kept hold of her arse with one hand, not allowing her to step backward or fall onto the bed. Her desire climbed to an absolute need.

She grabbed his chin and forced him to look up at her. "Bed. Now."

He nodded once, snatched her like she didn't weigh what she did, and then they were on the bed and he was poised at her entrance. The air seemed to shake with the thread of their mate bond. She couldn't see that thread, but she felt it as surely as she felt his body leaning into hers. It was bright, hot, and powerful. He cupped the back of her head and kissed her forehead, then he drove into her with one great thrust. Sparks of pure delight showered over her body, every inch of her linked to him in a way that was invisible to the eye but clear to the soul. Driving forward again and again, he angled himself so that he also pressed against her in exactly the right way. His hand smoothed quickly down her side to lift her leg onto his shoulder. The rightness of their fit had her biting her knuckles to keep from crying out.

"Tell me I am your mate, Tahlia," he said, quietly, his voice a snarl. His hair had fallen in a Fae-white sheet over half his face and he looked like a gorgeous, monstrous dream.

"I am your mate, Marius," she whispered huskily. "Yours. And you are mine."

Her pleasure rose to a point and exploded across her body, sending her into a moan she couldn't hold back as she rode the wave of sensation. Marius held a hand to her mouth and drove harder into her, his gaze pinning her in place as surely as his physical presence.

His head fell back and he shuddered, his body spasming.

"My lady. My Lady of the Skies. My Tahlia…"

The way he said her name with such reverence brought her back to another peak of pleasure and she shattered against him as he held still and hard inside her. At the last second, he worked her again and the second peak went on and on. She couldn't breathe for the joy and delight flooding her. He dropped down beside her, took her jaw between his thumb and forefinger, and turned her to face him. Her cheeks were blazing from exertion. He kissed her cheek, chin, and neck.

With each new kiss, he whispered a word of love and dedication. "Mine. My sweet. Perfection. I am yours. Only you see my heart, own my heart, are my heart."

And even though they would be braving unthinkable terrors quite soon, Tahlia fell into a dreamless sleep in her commander's arms.

CHAPTER 15

# TAHLIA

Tahlia woke in what felt like the middle of the night, though it was impossible to tell in this windowless room. A nightmare about dark waves and claws had ripped apart the peace she'd felt when she'd fallen asleep in Marius's arms. Blowing out a shaking breath, she tried to calm her heart. Swallowing her fear, she lit the candle on the bedside table and took one of Fara's letters. Lying stomach down, Marius snored lightly beside her.

*Dearest feral friend who refuses to have a normal job,*

*How are things going? I'll assume you still have both of your eyeballs since you are reading this. That's good. You must have avoided the human water. Is their wine any good? I doubt it.*

*ARE they handsy when they drink? I feel like I've heard they are. If any of those arseheads say a single thing to you that you don't like, just keep a list and some descriptions. I'll visit and undo their good health with great pleasure.*

*I HAVE A BROKEN HAND, by the way. I hid it from you when you were prepping to leave. I broke it on Anslem's face. He is a prickbrain. I do not regret it. I won't tell you what he said because it'll only get me riled up again, and I'm trying to study.*

*YES, prickbrain is a word. You can look it up in the library when you get back.*

*YOUR FRIEND,*
   *Fara*

CHUCKLING, Tahlia blew out the candle and settled back under the blanket with Marius. She curled her body around his, soaking in the heat and solidity of him. His scent filled the air and she fell asleep with the thought that someday soon she'd be surrounded by Fara and the other knights, that Lija would be healed, and all would be well.

Tahlia woke to Marius gently shaking her arm. He stood over her, dressed and ready.

"It's time," he whispered.

Behind him, the guard with the dark eyes stood waiting, lines forming between her eyebrows.

After a quick chug of watered wine and gobbling down another corncake, Tahlia followed Marius and the guard out of the room and into the corridor. The dawn's first gray light slid through archways in the passageway. The place was quiet as a tomb, but that was a good thing. It meant King Crazy was likely asleep and his cronies gone for the time being.

The guard stopped at the end of the third corridor they'd hurried down. This one bent sharply to the right. "Down there. Third door. You can't miss it."

"And our two are in place?" Marius glanced at Tahlia, then looked her up and down as if cataloging her breathing, stance, and general level of preparedness.

The guard breathed out, then pursed her lips. "As far as I know, one is on duty. Hopefully, both, but we couldn't ask because there wasn't any clear moment to do so without raising suspicion."

"Understood," Marius said.

"May the Old Ones bless you," the guard whispered quickly before heading off.

Keeping her steps as light as possible, Tahlia trailed Marius through the shadows that the fire from the wall sconces tried to shatter. Golden runes glimmered above one of the doorways. The entrance was housed in an alcove. This had to be the one. The guards were likely right on the other side of the heavy oak.

Marius turned the doorknob.

A guard with a beard rushed out, opening the door outward and slamming it against Marius.

"Filthy Fae spies," the man hissed as he lunged for Tahlia.

Marius was pinned to the alcove wall.

Tahlia bent to grab the dagger from her boot. Pulse flying as fast as Lija on a clear day, she shot upward, jamming the blade into the bearded guard's throat. Gurgling, he dropped, and Marius slid out from behind the door and began dragging him into the room they'd just opened. The other guard, the one presumably on their side, looked from Marius to Tahlia, then grabbed the dead guard's leg. He helped Marius hide the body behind a row of boxes.

The guard shoved his shoulder-length red hair out

of his face, then tugged a linen cloth from his belt and started back toward the door.

"I'll get the blood cleaned up. That guy was such an arsehole. Glad to see the last of him. Durniad was his hero."

"How did he know about us?" Tahlia cleaned her knife on her trousers, then returned it to the sheath sewn into the inside of her boot.

"He was your man until last night."

"Oh?" Marius's face was flat, emotionless as he knocked on the green-painted flagstones that made a half circle at the next door—the entrance to the labyrinth. What was he thinking? Did he not trust this guard?

"Yes, he was down here late last night," the guard said, "and when I showed back up this morning, he said Durniad had changed his mind. That he had it all wrong and that I had better get back on the right side of things or he'd kill me too. Didn't manage that now, did you?" The guard snorted and laughed.

"Do you think Durniad used the crown on him?" Tahlia asked.

Marius found the right stone and pushed one side. The stone tilted, and Marius reached into the space below it.

The guard shrugged. "It's possible, I guess. But Durniad is a great public speaker. He can charm anyone—even those he is about to kill in cold blood."

"It's a wonder he thinks he needs the crown," Tahlia said.

Marius made a *hmm* sound as he pulled a sack from the hidden spot on the floor. Tahlia joined in and they found lock-picking tools, small squares of linen, a tiny crock of grease, and a palm-sized book. Tahlia took that one up and flipped through the old vellum pages.

"Unseelie runes?" What in the world were these doing here?

Marius cut his eyes to her, telling her to keep quiet. "We are good here. Will you watch from the outside and give us a shout if anyone is coming?"

"I'll do what I can. I hate Durniad. Good luck to you."

Marius tipped his head at the human male. They divvied out the items their contacts had provided, tucking them into the leather pouches at their belts, in boots, and wherever else things would fit well enough.

"I feel like a walking craftsman's market," Tahlia said.

The weight of the rune book and the little lock pick hammer were too much for the loose waistband of her trousers. She tightened her belt another notch to keep the lot of it from falling to her ankles.

She glared at Marius over her shoulder. "No chuckling. Small but fierce, remember?"

He used to chide her for even wanting to be a

dragon rider because of her size. She'd proven to him that she was a fantastic flyer and fighter despite her petite build, but sometimes, he still smirked at her inability to reach the top shelf in their chambers at Dragon Tail.

"We have no time to lose," he said, pushing through the labyrinth's door. "Time to figure out these traps. Stay close. I don't want any more blood spilled if we can help it."

His voice sounded strained. She frowned as she followed him into complete darkness.

"Should I not have killed the bearded guard?" Her question bounced off the walls, walls that felt close.

"You did the right thing. He was going to snap your neck. There wasn't time for anything else. I've seen humans snap necks for lesser crimes than espionage and theft."

Torches set high into the walls around the room flickered to life, and Tahlia blinked against the sudden brightness. She took a breath, nodding to herself about what Marius had said. That was what she'd thought—that the killing was necessary. It wasn't her first time killing, but the act certainly wasn't the norm for her day. Thankfully, the experience with Ophelia and the monster Katk had warmed her up to violence.

The firelight showed a high stone ceiling above them and head-high walls at either side of them, close-set and quite obviously the labyrinth itself.

"We're already inside," she whispered, her stomach flipping with the knowledge that anything could come at them at any moment. She got out her knife again and savored the feel of Marius's powerful presence in front of her.

"Yes, and I assume we have stepped on a plate of sorts that triggered the lighting of the torches."

"How would that work?" Tahlia asked.

Marius made a grumbling noise. "Mechanisms that are worth a king's sum, I'm sure."

"Have you seen anything like this before?"

"No, but I've heard stories of the old kings and queens who ruled here," Marius said. "This wild setup isn't purely of Durniad's mind. This place was built ages ago. Before I was born. Durniad has simply fancied it up for us."

Fancied it up. Tahlia snickered. Marius was beginning to sound like her.

"How kind of him."

Marius harrumphed. "Indeed."

"So we have no idea what we're facing here, aside from the siren, right?" Tahlia's throat was dry as bone dust. She swallowed and fought a cough.

"We know there are traps. More than one. I would assume the siren wouldn't be the first."

Tahlia grinned wryly. "Ah, thinking like a madman, are you?"

Marius's left eyebrow flicked upwards. "One must

see through the eyes of the enemy to know his next move."

"Perhaps the first two traps will be simple for us since we're Fae."

"Perhaps," Marius said. "Perhaps not. We don't know if the guard we took out talked to Durniad about our plan."

"I don't love how much we are clueless about in here."

Marius growled in the way that meant he agreed.

"Do you realize you have five different growls in your vocabulary?"

He made no response except to shake his head and exhale.

"One tells the recipient to back off. Immediately." Tahlia pressed a hand to her chest. "I love that one."

"You do?"

"It's delightfully scary."

"You are very strange, my gorgeous mate."

Tahlia couldn't fight a smile. "Another of your growls indicates frustration with the situation at hand. Most would curse and swear in place of that growl."

"How much longer is this incredibly informative lesson going to last? We need to focus, little salty."

"Growl number three is for me."

"Oh, yes? How so?"

She stepped closer and ran a hand up his thigh. He

stopped, looked over his shoulder at her, and growled as the torchlight flickered in his eyes. Her body grew as hot as the flames lighting the labyrinth.

"Yes, that one."

He started walking again, shaking her off. "It's impressive that we can feel lusty at this dire moment."

"Well, you know what they say about newlyweds."

He frowned, eyeing her. "No, what do they say? Is this a human saying?"

"Oh, no, I don't think so," she said. "I don't remember where I heard it."

"Eh, why don't you walk beside me? I don't like you out of my sight like this."

"All right." She came up next to him and he lifted her hand. He sniffed her knuckles. "What is it? Oh, the blood. From the guard. I didn't get it all off."

His steps slowed, and he stared at her blood-stained hand, his gaze distant.

"Marius, what's wrong?"

# CHAPTER 16

# MARIUS

A memory of his sister flashed through his mind. She was screaming as a human cut her down outside their home. The human pirate slashed at her again and again and...

No, that wasn't a memory.

It was how Marius had imagined her death all these years. She had been killed in that way, so the report said. But he hadn't witnessed the crime. If he'd been there, he would have defended his sister and it would have been the human's head on the ground instead of hers.

"Marius?"

He blinked the vibrant imagining away to see Tahlia's eyes. Well, they weren't her eyes, exactly. The Witch's potion remained in place, rounding her irises.

This was Tahlia's human face, her human eyes. This was what Tahlia was without the half of her blood that was Fae.

His stomach rolled and he turned away, gasping. Gods, what was wrong with him? What did that have to do with anything? Why was he having pseudo-flashbacks?

"I'm sorry. I'm…" He gritted his teeth and faced Tahlia. "I had a memory, or no, a thought about my sister."

"The one who was killed by pirates."

"Aye. I only had the one." He cleared his throat.

"Are you all right? What can I do to help?"

Marius's heart melted. She was perfect. "There's nothing you need to do. Obviously, I have very complicated feelings regarding being around humans. I'm also wound up because that guard tried to kill you. It's difficult being on a mission with you as my bonded mate. "

She grabbed him around the middle as if they weren't in a madman's labyrinth with only the gods knew what facing them very shortly. He wrapped his arms around her and breathed in her scent. After a count of three, he released her.

"I can't be this selfish. We must move on, and I need to stop being foolish. You are a knight and I am your commander. I can't let myself falter."

"You are allowed to have feelings."

"Not on a mission," he said.

"But what if said emotions motivate you to fight to the best of your ability?"

He growled. She made a decent point.

"See? You agree. That's the agree growl."

"Please stop cataloguing my sounds."

"Hmm. I don't know. How about you let me if I let you take notes on my noises when we get home," she whispered, her tone sending all his blood south of his belt.

"Focus. Please."

"Yes, sir."

"That's better."

They walked on, the labyrinth taking them down neat ninety-degree turns and the torches giving just enough light to see.

A bang and a shuffling sound broke the silence. Tahlia immediately whirled to press her back to his so they were facing opposite directions and ready for a fight. He was glad to know her training had sunk in so effectively already.

"What is that?" Tahlia kept her voice to a whisper.

A rumbling shook the walls around them.

"Perhaps the storm they said was coming has landed."

"Hell of a storm."

"They do see some rough ones similar to those up north of us on the pirate coast." The moment the word *pirate* was out of his mouth, he wished he hadn't spoken it. He wanted to wash that imagined memory from his head and crush the dark feelings it grew inside him.

Tahlia resumed her spot beside him until the labyrinth narrowed—the first thing to change about the place. She stepped behind him. "Still want to lead?"

"Yes, I'm guessing any attack will come from where we haven't yet been," he said.

"You're the—"

Her word slurred into a gasp and Marius spun to see the floor under her give way. She disappeared into the black space below.

Heart locked in ice, he lunged for her, but he was far too late. A stale wind blew up from the hole in the floor. On his knees at the opening in the ground, he searched the darkness, but he couldn't see a thing.

"Tahlia!"

No sound. No answer.

He couldn't move. Breathing was a forgotten skill. His heart wasn't even beating.

If she was...

He pressed his eyes shut and shook his head. Forcing himself to breathe and think, he opened his eyes again.

"I'm coming down," he said into the dark.

A quiet snarl made him lift his head to look down the labyrinth's path.

*No, it couldn't be.* Gods, save him and Tahlia both.

# CHAPTER 17

# TAHLIA

The dark was like a second skin, so tightly woven and pressed against Tahlia with not an inch of wiggle room. Not even the hole she'd fallen through was visible. Where was the torchlight? Pain reverberated through her bones like the storm's thunder had crawled inside her body.

Grunting, she tried to sit up. Her fingers found a spongy surface. She tore a handful of whatever it was away from the solid ground and sniffed it. Moss. Not moss like they had in the Realm of Lights and the Shrouded Mountains, but something grittier and less leafy. Definitely moss though.

"Thank you, moss. You saved my life."

Without the heavy coating of the stuff, the hard earth would have cracked her skull in two. She was glad to have Fae strength. A human with no Fae blood would have been destroyed by that drop.

She looked up, not that the dark was any different up than down. Longing to call out for Marius, she opened her mouth, but then thought better of it. What if there was something down here and her shout made it attack? What if she was now in an area where Durniad's guards would hear her? Maybe that was why he wasn't calling down to her. But then again, if she was close enough to hear him, she'd see the torchlight.

Gods, what *was* this place? Was there a spell on the space that turned it into total darkness? Or had she somehow fallen so far as to be out of view of the hole and Marius?

Shaking the moss from her fingers, she began to check the extent of her injuries. A big lump on the back of her head. Her right ankle wasn't grand at the moment—hopefully just a mild sprain. She wasn't a healer, so she couldn't exactly fix it herself.

She spread a hand over her torso. Her shirt had come untucked and had ripped on one side. A cut bled lightly over her ribs. Her ribs were sore, but not broken, she didn't think. Oh, Fara's letters had slipped out of her waistband and the small belt bag that held the lock-picking items and a few odds and ins had torn away.

Getting onto her hands and knees, she felt around

the ground. The scent of the sea wafted across her face and she stilled.

A breeze meant an escape.

While crawling on the ground like a sad little bug wasn't her favorite activity, she stuck with the hands and knees set up because she was dizzy. Standing up only to fall again would be the height of stupidity.

Something crinkled under her fingers.

Fara's letters! Hope flooded her. Just the idea of having Fara's writing with her now was a blessing. Her bag and the rest of her stuff were a shuffle away. She tied the pouch around her stomach, making do with the torn edges of the strap. Adjusting her belt over her tunic again, she was as put together as she could be, considering. The cut on her side flared with pain, but there wasn't much to do about it now, so she continued toward the direction of the sea breeze.

What was Marius doing? Would he try to come down here to get her? She hoped not. Fear gripped her mind, and she crawled faster, determined to fight its hold on her. If only she hadn't lost her Weaver magic when she'd crossed the Veil...

Maybe she could find it, activate it, whatever. But how?

No, she'd find the opening where that breeze was coming from. She'd get through it and somehow get back to Marius and the search for the crown.

And then a very hard surface cracked her against

the head. Her brain felt like it was about to pour out her ears.

"Ugh."

She rubbed at yet another lump on her head, then looked up. Reaching up a hand, she wiggled her fingers in hopes of feeling the sea air.

A breath of the outdoors danced over her fingertips and she scrambled to her feet. Dizziness pulled at her, but she braced herself against the wall that had so unjustifiably attacked her.

"The least you can do is hold me up, wall. This is your doing."

Hmm. Was she woozy? Why was she talking to a wall?

Running her palm up the rough stone and patchy moss, she found a hole. She could fit exactly zero parts of her into said opening.

Dammit.

She sat down to cry. Because honestly, she needed to get it out of the way. Her head was killing her. Maybe if she wept for a bit, she'd have the mind to work up another plan.

Pressing her hands over her eyes, she let the tears roll.

"I refuse to have a pity party, but this is decidedly not knightlike, this whole falling in a hole to die alone and filthy thing."

A prickling sensation spread across Tahlia's scalp and into her ears. She shivered. What in the...

"Tahlia?" A quiet voice, like someone very far away, echoed in her ears. "Tahlia."

Tahlia sat up straight, her eyes going dry immediately. "Who said that?"

The voice was familiar...

# CHAPTER 18

# MARIUS

The minotaur launched itself at Marius, who shook himself and began to run.

A minotaur? Even more than sirens, he'd thought minotaurs were a thing of imagination. At least the bottom half was human. Surely he, a full Fae, could outrun it. But what then? Keep running until it tired, go for a kill? But how long would that leave Tahlia beneath the labyrinth? He had to get to her. This place was making it incredibly difficult to remain logical. None of this seemed real.

He longed for his dragon and his whip as well, but as he had known for quite a while now, longing didn't kill the pirate or monster or minotaur.

Action did.

With the grunting bull creature not five steps behind him, he turned sharply and made to speed past it and run in the opposite direction. If anything, he had to keep his hold on where Tahlia had fallen. They had to have passed it. Why hadn't either of them fallen through?

Roaring, the mythical beast gave chase and Marius kept a keen eye on the path.

But the hole wasn't there. All the stones were smooth, unmarred and unbroken, as if Tahlia and her drop had all been in his imagination.

He whirled and kicked toward the minotaur's chest. His boot made contact and the creature howled, dropped back, and made to lunge, but Marius was faster. Marius drove his blade into the bull-headed thing's eye. Hot blood gushed over his hand, but the minotaur shook and pierced Marius's shoulder with the tip of a horn. Pain spread out in a web over Marius and he grunted, angry. He tore the knife from the minotaur's eye and jammed it into the beast's neck.

The minotaur disappeared.

What in the name of all the gods?

# CHAPTER 19
## TAHLIA

"You know who this is, you fantastic idiot," the voice said. "I can't believe this is working!"

Tahlia's tears returned and brought loads of company. "Fara!"

She slapped her hands over her mouth, worried her shout would bring out something she didn't have the balance to fight right now.

"What's working? Am I hallucinating?" Tahlia whispered.

"No, it's Fara! Lija and I are with Healer Albus and an herbwitch from the south."

Tahlia's heart lurched and her eyes burned with tears. Lija. Fara. She grasped at her tunic, her pulse pounding like her heart might beat right through the fabric.

"Fara," she said, voice cracking. "I want to know everything, but currently, I'm stuck in a very deep, probably cursed hole under a madman's fortress. I might die." An unhinged laugh bubbled from her. "Like soon. Lija, I miss you. I hate being so far from you. Fara, can you make it so I can talk to Marius?"

"Hello, rider," Lija said.

Her voice was low and soft, comforting but edged with desperation. This wasn't like the experience of speaking mentally; this was like Lija was nearby and Tahlia could simply hear her. So fascinating!

But despite the joy of this magic, Tahlia could easily tell that Lija wanted to hide how poorly she felt. Not being able to fly truly was bringing her down.

"I'm going to finish this thing and get you healed, Lija."

"I believe it."

A tear tracked down Tahlia's flushed cheeks. "Fara, can I contact Marius?"

"He isn't with you?"

"No. Only I fell. And for some reason, I can't even see the hole I fell through nor can I shout up to Marius. If up is even truly up here..."

"Gods, that sounds terrifying. All right. Hold on."

"Can this herbwitch heal Lija?"

"No, she tried. She says she isn't very powerful and her talent sits mainly in communication so she was thrilled to find this rare herb that facilitated this due to your soul bond with Lija and—"

"Fara. Please. I don't know how much time I have. Marius is assuredly desperate and searching for me, which will make him vulnerable to attack. For all I know, he is dealing with a siren right now."

Fara swore creatively. "I thought sirens had gone extinct."

"I thought they were never real."

"Hold on, sorry. Just a minute," Fara said.

The sensation of the magic they were working rushed over Tahlia's scalp again.

"Try now," Fara said, her voice going in and out.

Saying a silent prayer, Tahlia took a breath. "Marius?"

There was a grunt of surprise, then silence.

"Marius, it's Tahlia. Fara and her gang are doing some sort of communication magic. It's really me. Ask me anything." If it was even working... What if it wasn't him she was talking to?

"Tahlia." His voice flooded her with warmth from the top of her head to the very tip of her toes. "Where are you? Are you hurt? Are you able to communicate with them and with me due to your Weaver magic?"

"No. It has to do with Fara and Lija. I'll explain later. I fell into a dark cavern of sorts. There is a small hole in the far wall down here, and I smell the sea.

Sadly, I can't see the hole I fell through. I think this is a cursed or spelled area."

"Agreed. I can't find the broken path you fell through on this side either. There are Unseelie runes everywhere in this damned fortress. Idiot humans messing with powers they can't possibly understand."

"Yes, yes," she said. "Berate them at your leisure once you get me out of the very scary hole, agreed?"

"I would begin working on that if I weren't currently on top of the labyrinth wall, trying my best to find a minotaur that apparently is capable of portalling from one place to another as he sees fit."

"I'm sorry. What?"

"You heard me correctly. Half-human. Half-bull. Disappearing and potentially reappearing. Even grouchier than I am, if one can believe that."

Tahlia laughed darkly. "I'm glad you've adopted my whole humor-in-the-face-of-death practice. Do you have a guess on where the minotaur is right now? I can't believe we have to deal with not one, but two mythical dangers on the same mission. This is too much. I want a raise."

Marius growled. "I heard a noise in that direction," he said pointing farther into the labyrinth. "Could be the minotaur. But something is very off here, Lady Tahlia."

"So many somethings are off."

"I'm going to attempt to kill the minotaur, and then I'll drive through the damn floor and get to you."

"Sounds lovely. Happy hunting, dear," she said, hoping her teasing tone covered the fear inching up her back like a horribly large spider. She took a shuddering breath.

Marius's grumble faded into the recesses of her ears as Fara's voice came through once more.

"Did it work?" Fara asked. "Did you cut him off yourself?"

"I think so? I have no clue how this is working."

"The herbwitch said something about intention and need."

"Fine. Whatever. Can she tell me how to get my Weaver magic back out here past the Veil?"

"Let me ask," Fara said.

Tahlia frowned into the dark. "Are you eating?"

"Just a crystal cake. Look, I need energy to help you, all right?"

Tahlia snorted and shook her head, but she wasn't irritated. She was just so glad not to be alone in the dark. She took another deep inhale of the sea breeze and tried not to panic about being stuck and about Marius battling a bull-man.

"Have you tried meditating to try to get your weird little lines back?" Fara asked.

"No, my head is just now clearing from the hard hit when I fell, and there hasn't been time for it in the chaos of this city. You should see the humans, Fara. They're so relaxed and always laughing."

"Well, you're seeing them during a festival."

"I think they're like this though. Full of jokes and not nearly as uptight as us Fae."

"Us Fae?"

"You know I always felt more Fae than human," Tahlia said.

"Do you still feel that way?" Fara asked.

Tahlia chewed the inside of her cheek. Maybe not. Maybe she did feel more of a natural connection to these humans. "I'm not sure. Let's move on to this meditation idea."

"All right. So in Healer training, they taught me that slow, steady breathing actually lowers your heart rate and helps you think more clearly. Perhaps that would help your magic?"

"I'll give it a go. Will you stay with me?" Tahlia hated that she sounded so needy, but losing a chunk of her pride was nothing to being alone in the dark.

"We aren't going anywhere," Lija said, speaking over Fara shouting, "Of course!"

A smile pulled at Tahlia's lips, and she sat up. "Any tips on how to do this?"

"Sit with a straight spine if you're able," Fara said. "How are your injuries at the moment?"

"I'll live. All right, I'm sitting. What else?"

"Breathe in for four counts, hold it for four, release

it in four counts, then pause for four, and begin again. Close your eyes."

"It's so dark. It won't make much of a difference."

"It cues your body to relax because everyone closes their eyes to sleep."

"I can sleep with my eyes open," Lija said, her voice sounding a little farther away than Fara's now.

"To watch for predators," Tahlia added, feeling a glimmer of Lija's pride through their bond. "I felt your pride, Lija! Maybe this aural connection makes it possible for us to examine one another. Can you tell if I have any serious internal injuries?"

Lija made a low growling sound and Tahlia knew what she was thinking. "I sense pain," the dragon said, "but nothing that will stop you from getting out of there and back home to me."

Tahlia chuckled. "Spot on." She closed her eyes. "I'm going to begin now. I hope I'm facing the place where I fell so maybe something will come to me and show me how to escape. It's tough to tell direction down here."

And it was tough not giving up. Tahlia swallowed and breathed in slowly.

*Hold on, Marius. Just stay alive.*

# CHAPTER 20

# MARIUS

Marius crept down the top of the labyrinth's wall, keeping his steps completely silent. Breathing sounded a short way down the labyrinth. It had to be the minotaur... Unless there was another massive mouth-breathing monster down here. It was possible, but he certainly hoped it was just the one beast.

The tops of the minotaur's horns showed above the third turn past where they had been fighting. Marius's heart lifted. It was injured. He could finish the job now and go back to helping Tahlia.

But that was odd... The air didn't smell of blood. The beast had definitely been bleeding from the eye wound. At least, the fluid had been red like a basic creature's blood, and it had smelled as such at the moment. Perhaps the minotaur was capable of more than portalling from one spot to another.

He took as deep a breath as he dared, not wanting to alert the creature in this tomb-like silence. There was an occasional noise, like a bang and a murmur, far off, but that wouldn't cover Marius's sounds this close to the minotaur.

He crept closer, closer still. The beast's scent—like any barn animal's homely smell—touched Marius's nose.

Marius leapt from the wall and rammed his blade into the base of the minotaur's head. The creature shoved backward, crushing Marius between beast and wall. Marius swore, pain lashing through his spine. With a mighty roar, the minotaur shook itself. Marius held on, eardrums buzzing and cracking with the minotaur's noise. The agony of being crushed grew to a point that seemed deadly. Shouting out in desperation and frustration, Marius pushed the blade in further. The minotaur dropped. Exhaling a gust of pained breath, Marius fell with him, but...

The minotaur blinked out of existence.

Marius snarled and lifted his weapon. There wasn't even a speck of blood on the blade. It was madness! His mind whirled and he gritted his teeth. What was happening here? What was he missing? He'd thought the traps would be primarily physical until the siren, but this...

Wait.

The siren. What were sirens capable of exactly? In the stories, they were so beautiful that those attracted to the female form were drawn into the water the sirens inhabited. Some tales claimed sirens were half-fish while others said half-bird. All had elements of song to the myth, and many included illusions. He assumed the siren would make herself appear as the victim's most desired form, but perhaps there was more to the creature's powers. Perhaps a siren could make him see a minotaur and fail to see a hole in the floor.

He hurried back to where Tahlia had disappeared. Kneeling, he felt around for any break in the stones, anything off at all. The path was smooth though. He reached farther, then his hand dropped, and he nearly tumbled through a break in the labyrinth's floor. There it was. As plain as the sun in the sky, though this was black as night. He could see the ground, wet and rough.

"Tahlia?" he called out as loud as he dared.

He didn't wish to alert the siren if his guess was correct and she'd been the one creating the illusion. If she found out he'd broken the magic, surely she'd be angered and perhaps she'd come for him. He needed time to help Tahlia.

Praying, he called for Tahlia again, this time a bit louder. Should he drop into the hole himself or would that be ruining their chance at success here? He looked around, wishing he had something—anything—that could serve as a rope. He could rip his clothing into strips. *Yes, that might work.*

Or should he leap into the hole?

He could see the ground at the base of the hole, and even with his Fae blood, he wouldn't be able to handle that drop without risking injury. No, he had to be smart here and not let the feral side of him panic for fear of his mate. He bridled his growing alarm and put his meager plan into practice, calling out for Tahlia between his quick ripping and braiding work. He only needed the lower half of his trousers. They were double-layered.

A great howling echoed through the labyrinth, raising the hairs on Marius's arms. What was that? Gods, they had to get this job finished and get out. Who knew what other horrors awaited them in this terrible place?

He went back to fixing the rope, constantly debating whether he should make it thicker or longer and which would help her more.

After a few minutes of braiding, he finally finished. He removed two of the blades he had stashed in his uniform and knotted each end of the rope around one of the sheathed weapons. A space about a hand's wide had opened up between the cobblestones that made up the labyrinth's floor. He wedged one blade into the space, securing the rope. Tugging, he tested the blade and knot's position to see if it would hold Tahlia. Satisfied, he dropped the other end into the hole.

"Tahlia! I've lowered a rope down. Can you hear me? Tahlia?" He dared to call out a bit louder this time.

Then his ears began to buzz. A song filled his head. Chimes. Bells. A voice so clear and full of mourning that tears burned his eyes.

"What are you doing, Fae male?" a light voice asked a few steps down the labyrinth's path.

He turned but could only see a shadowy silhouette. But she was the one singing.

"I fashioned a rope," he answered, not at all concerned.

"Why?"

"To help Tahlia free herself." His head swam, and he rubbed a hand over his face quickly to try to clear his mind.

"Hmm." The melodious voice sounded closer though the speaker didn't appear to have moved. "Come with me. You won't need to worry about rope or her with me."

"But she needs me. And I, her."

"I doubt that. Come," she sang. "Come with me."

Each time she sang the words *come with me,* a breeze fluttered through Marius's half-bound hair and the scent of brine filled the air. He remembered a day long in the past, a day that honestly he might have invented, something that wasn't a true event and only real in his imaginings. But in this makeshift memory, he stood beside his sister, hand in hand, and they stared at the sea. There were no fires in the cliffside fortress or pirates firing arrows from their quick ships. Only the rolling waves, a soft wind, and the scent of sand and sea. It was before he had known much about the world at large, back when everything felt safe.

"Come with me, Marius," she sang, the song unfurling in his blood and making him feel as light as air.

Pleasure and anticipation danced through his veins. He looked up and realized he was standing instead of sitting beside the hole where Tahlia had fallen. A figure stood beside him, her eyes trained on a pointed archway opening to a low roof that hung over a sloping stretch of black sand.

"How do you know my name?" he asked, turning to face the figure.

Swiftly flowing water covered every inch of her skin. He looked her up and down, unable to stop his lips parting in shock and wonder. No, the water *was* her skin. Beds of kelp, coral shelves, and schools of fish lived in her skin. The scale altered from one moment to the next with the fish and kelp looking miniature now and then full scale somehow. He shook his head, dizzy with the impossibility of what he was seeing. Her watery flesh held in a heart as bright as a gold coin and lungs as red as rubies. She was made of the sea's treasure—both natural and lost in shipwrecks. The female was gorgeous, but his mind couldn't comprehend her in full.

His gaze slid to her face. "Your eyes…"

They were topaz—copper and sea blue. It was like they laughed at his wonder, but how could eyes laugh like that? The sound of her voice chimed in his ears. He growled in frustration, but the song crashed into him anyway, turning everything to bliss. A soft hand tugged at his hand, and the black sand was pleasantly gritty beneath his bare feet.

When had he removed his boots?

When had he left the labyrinth and decided to follow this female made of sea and treasure?

"Come with me," she sang again, and that breeze and those feelings once again swept across him and burned his worries into ash.

All worries and every thought besides the sea melted from his mind as they left the dark and sandy corridor and approached the easy waves of the shoreline. He sighed and went with the being into the ocean, delighting in the feel of the cool water lapping at his knees. They walked slowly until the water was chest-high.

"Be still," the female said.

He obeyed, and she passed a hand over his face.

Then she pulled him under.

CHAPTER 21

# TAHLIA

Tahlia was free from the dark hole and back in the labyrinth.

But Marius was gone.

*Damn.* If she had her Weaver magic, she might be able to track him. But she'd tried the four-count breathing as Fara had instructed, in and out, with all the ridiculous holding and everything. But no magic had sparkled over her head or eyes or whatever. No, she'd found a rope though, and she was out of the hole. She assumed Marius had made the rope out of his clothing because his scent had drawn her through the inky darkness to the rope's braided fabric.

She lifted her nose, trying to scent Marius again, to see if anything led her the way he'd gone. But no, her nose was good, but not full-Fae-blood good.

"I really hope I don't run into a minotaur right now. My ankle and ribs are still killing me. At least my head is feeling better."

Lija's voice mumbled through Tahlia's mind. Tension tightened Tahlia's shoulders and neck. She couldn't stand to lose her aural connection to Fara and Lija when Marius was missing.

"I couldn't hear that," she said quietly, hoping the mythological beasts roaming this madhouse wouldn't be alerted. "Can you speak up or toss some more of that herb into the mix?"

"Rider, do you hear me now?"

"Ah, much better, yes."

"Lady Fara is threatening the visiting herbwitch."

Oh, no. "Why?"

"She said if this connection fails before you catch up with Marius, she'll, and I quote, 'String your yarrow-scented intestines over the castle walls.'"

Tahlia bit her lip to keep her laugh quiet. "Tell her to behave. She might ruin her chances at becoming a full-fledged Healer if she does too much eviscerating."

Lija's chuckle was music to Tahlia's ears.

Wait. "I heard music while I was climbing out. Did you hear any of that? It was very faint. Felt off."

"I didn't," Lija said.

"Me neither," Fara said, her voice coming back and overlapping Lija's. "And don't you worry about me and my situation back here. Not your business, you wonderful, death-wish-having maniac. You are my priority."

"Thanks, Fara." Her heart warmed and she walked farther into the labyrinth. "I think that space under this labyrinth was cloaked in a spell because I couldn't even see the opening I was climbing out of until I was nearly free. And the music..."

A chill swept over her. "Oh, no."

"What is it?" Lija asked.

"The music I heard," Tahlia said, "I bet it was the siren."

Fara was swearing before Tahlia had finished her sentence. "...and that cock-brained arse with—"

"Fara. Calm down. Please. I need to think. If Marius was here setting up the rope for me..." Tahlia absently touched the two blades she'd untangled from the rope's end knots. "And the siren appeared." She exhaled slowly, trying to feel anger rather than fear. "Well, I guess we know where Marius went."

"I can help," Lija said. "I've lived near sirens. Long ago, during my youngling stage."

"I had no idea. I thought you were born in the Shrouded Mountains like the other mountain dragons."

"I was born near Dragon Tail Peak, but Seabreaks usually visit the sea to swim before reaching adulthood. It's a rite of passage."

"Fascinating." Lija's information helped Tahlia keep her panic at bay. "Tell me more."

The labyrinth met the wall of the massive chamber then turned to the left. In the wall, an opening the size of a double doorway shimmered.

"Wait. There's a magical opening here. It could be a portal. It's definitely been created with magic."

"That will be her entry to the sea. Sirens can remove stone like a splash of water clears mud if they are motivated to do so."

Black sand lined the ground beyond the hole in the labyrinth wall. Two sets of footprints marked the sand. One was a slender barefoot print about the size of Tahlia's foot and the other showed what had to be Marius's boot print. The sound of the ocean whispered down the sandy, cave-like corridor.

"All right. I'm following footprints. I'm fairly certain one set of these is Marius's."

"Whatever you do, rider, make certain the siren doesn't see you. They won't smell you in the water. Their sense of smell is one of their weaknesses."

"That's very good to know."

The sand crunched beneath Tahlia's feet as she hurried down the black sand and into a breeze that grew saltier with every step. The corridor opened up to a rocky beach. Pale cliffs towered behind Tahlia and the foamy waves lapped the shore at the toes of her boots. The waves were growing larger and wilder, like gray hands clapping and grasping at the lowering clouds. Lightning cracked overhead and thunder shook the beach as the smell of rain filled the air.

"I don't see them anywhere."

"She has taken him under already?" Lija asked. Voices spoke in the background.

"Yes. Unless I'm wrong, and he hasn't been swayed by her at all. Maybe he's back in the labyrinth. Yeah, perhaps I should head back inside and make sure he isn't just around another corner or two."

"If she has claimed him, you have very little time to catch up to them before they disappear for good."

Tahlia gritted her teeth and fisted her hands. "But he isn't currently drowning if he's down there with her, right? Please tell me that, at least."

"No, she won't let him drown before she entertains herself with him."

And then she spotted Marius's boots. A chill rocked her and she bent halfway, bracing herself on her knees. Swallowing against the lump in her throat, Tahlia tried not to panic.

"All right," she said, her voice shaky. "I'm going in. But it's not as if I swim regularly. I wish you were here, Lija. For many, many reasons."

"I do too, rider. I do too. Now, shake that despair off your shoulders, knight, and look around the shoreline for a palm-sized stone that has been smoothed from years of seaside existence."

"Why?"

"I'll explain as you search," Lija said.

The beach was a sea itself with pebbles stretching for a mile, maybe more. "Any palm-sized stone?"

"Yes. If it doesn't work the first time, we can try until it does."

"Try what?" At Tahlia's feet, a smooth, light brown stone reflected another strike of lightning. She picked it up. "Got a rock for you, my mysterious dragon."

"Good. Do you have a blade?"

"Several."

Lija's chuckle was dark and full of promised vengeance on those who went against them. "You'll need to carve four runes on the stone."

"But I don't have magic. I have no Unseelie blood." Some Seelie Fae did have Unseelie blood and were just recently being open about it. After discovering the link between Fae King Lysanael and the Unseelie realm, the stigma had faded somewhat. Only the humans' Witch and the Fae's Druid could do full magic in this realm— the world of Seelie Fae and humans.

"This is sea magic and you are bonded to a Seabreak, rider. Trust me."

"Do the other knights know about this magic of yours?"

"They've seen some of it in battle with Donan and

Lady Maiwenn, but they know enough not to ask too many questions about dragon business."

"Understood."

Lija began detailing the lines and shapes of the runes Tahlia had to carve. They went one by one, Lija explaining and Tahlia etching the magical symbols as clearly as possible on the stone.

"It's finished," Tahlia said, feeling shaky for a thousand reasons. The rain was cold. Marius was missing. Durniad would be claiming the crown and using it to wreak havoc on the entire world in a bit. She had injuries that burned and pulsed with pain. Oh, and she was about to hunt a siren.

"Sit as Lady Fara instructed you earlier. Hold the stone over your chest."

Tahlia didn't argue, but she did take a minute to strip off her boots as well as to remove her belt and Fara's letters. When she was in position with the stone against her chest, she checked in.

"I'm ready."

"Imagine that I am beside you and your hand is on my scales. Pretend as though we breathe in and out like we are the same creature."

A warmth traveled down Tahlia's head, shoulders, and chest. Her lungs, mouth, and nose tingled like they were going numb.

"Do you feel the magic, rider?"

"I do."

"Then you can enter the sea without worry for air. Leave the stone on the beach and let us begin our hunt."

Tahlia waded into the chilly, storm-tossed surf. The cliffs curved around the beach like a scythe. The tide tugged at her legs.

"Will the runes also help me swim in a storm like this?"

"You're stronger than you realize. Your bond with me has altered your body and your blood."

The water deepened and Tahlia began to swim. Maybe she truly could find Marius and help him escape the siren. Maybe Lija wasn't being insane.

"How does this hunt begin?" she asked, trying not to let fear roll over her like one of the sea's massive swells.

"Stop lollygagging and get on with it. Dive in, rider!"

"Bossy, aren't we?" Tahlia did as Lija ordered.

The water enveloped her and she parted her lips. Would she drown? No, Lija would protect her. She knew that.

Tahlia opened her mouth and inhaled. Her lungs expanded, pressing against the pain in her injured ribs. But the rune stone worked. She was breathing under water. Miraculous. But could she speak to Lija like this? She hadn't been able to speak inside the mind as she and Lija usually did. Communicating out loud had been an intuitive decision that had held. But maybe…

*Can you hear me, Lija?*

Tahlia swam forward and the water parted around her limbs like she'd been born a fish rather than a half-Fae. Wow.

"Can you see any bubbles as if something large is exhaling into the water?" Lija asked, her voice quiet but clear in Tahlia's ears.

Hoping this was going to work, Tahlia opened her mouth to speak. "Can you hear and understand me?" How could she? Tahlia's words were strangled by the water and she couldn't pronounce anything correctly.

"Well enough, rider. Well enough."

"Good. I see many bubbles."

"Keep swimming, my lady Tahlia," Lija said. "Look for a trail of bubbles in the shapes of feathers."

Feathers? Tahlia kept her eyes open, shocked that she could see clearly. Granted, the flash of lightning and the twist of the water altered the look of the sandy ocean floor, the waving kelp, and the two schools of fish—one silver and one poppy red—that swam by. But still, the details of a round coral bloom showed clearly despite appearing one hundred yards or so away.

She reached out her arms and kicked her feet in the cool water, her eyesight far sharper than it had ever been under water. The sea floor dropped, and a break of seagrass with bright gold flowers that shimmered with their own illumination ran in a curving path along the deepest cut in the ground. At the end of the seagrass, a line of elongated, soft-looking bubbles danced through the water toward the surface.

"Found them," she said as best she could with water chilling her mouth and salting her tongue.

"Good," Lija said. "The entrance to her lair is likely decorated in a way you won't miss."

"I don't like the sound of that."

"A fitting attitude when dealing with sirens. She is extremely dangerous, rider."

"Let's say I make it into her lair—what do I do then? I assume hand-to-hand combat isn't my best choice of action."

"No, unless you can break the hold she has on Marius. You two could probably best her physically. But not just you. She'll use him to get to you. And that's if you manage to surprise her before she can sing to you."

"So I am susceptible."

"Maybe less so because you find males attractive, but her power remains a definite threat."

"This whole *saving Marius from an evil female* is getting old, if I'm honest."

Lija huffed, dark amusement coming through their bond. "Let's hope you are saving him and not just tossing yourself into the tragedy."

Tahlia blew out a mouthful of bubbles. "Yes, let's hope for that," she said wryly.

They weren't so deep that light didn't penetrate the water here. Flashes of lightning danced through the salt water and helped Tahlia see.

She said a silent prayer and swam forward.

# CHAPTER 22

# MARIUS

The moment the ocean water hit Marius's face, his mind cleared. He swore viciously inside his head.

He'd been fooled by a siren.

They swam onward through a deep valley under the sea. He didn't dare alert the siren that he was aware of himself. How was he breathing down here? He had no recollection of leaving the labyrinth or arriving at the seaside.

The siren wasn't singing now. If she started up again, would he lose his senses? Maybe if he recreated his state of mind when his head cleared, he'd be able to do it again should the need arise. He recalled the chilly water and a bolt of protective desire for Tahlia. Their mating bond was powerful and the thought of her had forced the siren's magic from him. Were sirens aware of that? Considering he hadn't even realized sirens existed in today's world, he certainly didn't have a broad knowledge of their behavior, strengths, or weaknesses. This creature swimming beside him was an unknowable enemy. The worst type of opponent.

He longed to look around and make certain he knew the way back to shore. Not that he had a single idea on how to breathe under water long enough once he fought the siren and broke whatever magic she was wielding to keep him from drowning.

"Welcome to my home, Fae."

Her chiming voice threatened to pull his mind under again. He imagined the feel of Tahlia's cheek on his palm and the heat of her kiss. The siren's influence faded.

The inconsistent light of the storm above sent flashes of illumination through the water. They swam through a curtain of dark red kelp and into a cave with a wide opening on the far side. Sea creatures like snails gathered in clusters on the cave walls, their shells glowing as gold as the coins that made up the siren's heart. Something pale on the ground caught Marius's eye and he looked down to see a path of bones.

It was only his training that kept him from reacting and giving himself away. Some were the tiny bones of fish, their spines still intact. But others...

Human skulls, long femurs, and the unmistakable cages of ribs littered the lair.

Fear sliced across his thoughts, but he found the calm within him as he always did in terrible scenarios, and he schooled his features before she looked at him again. He had to get out of here. Now. Durniad would be coming for the crown soon. Tahlia had to escape the fortress before she was caught. He knew her enough to be certain she'd be searching for him if she managed to free herself with his rope. His fingers began to curl into fists, but he relaxed them and kept his gaze on the siren.

She eased him toward one of the cave's walls, singing as her palms pressed into his chest. Memories of his family flooded his mind; then there were memories that weren't real. He had no brother. Who was that? He visualized Tahlia laughing and the soft touch of her hand in his. The siren's manufactured memories faded from his mind's eye.

The siren plucked a pale orange berry from a plant growing along the cave's roof. She placed it between his lips.

"Eat this, Fae male. You will feel very good indeed if you do."

Her words, not sung exactly but lilting and song-like, warmed his ears and he relaxed more than he needed to.

*Tahlia. Tahlia, my mate,* he repeated silently to himself.

What would this berry do to him? Kill him? Put him to sleep so she could dine on his innards without a fuss? Gods, this was horrendous.

But what choice did he have? If he fought her, she might be stronger than him. Or she might negate whatever magic had him breathing here.

The siren parted his lips. "Open up, Fae."

Heart racing, Marius rammed his forehead into her nose. Blood bloomed around them, and he shot toward the lair's entrance as the siren shrieked. Her noise made his ears ring painfully. Swimming as quickly as he could, he breathed like some sort of magical fish, using his mouth, nose, and lungs still. Her magic hadn't broken with his strike.

But he knew without looking that the siren would be on him in moments despite her injury. He hurried, swimming as quickly as his limbs allowed.

He swam right into another person. Grunting, his eyes focused and...

It was Tahlia. No, she couldn't be here. He gripped her arm and started swimming again as the siren's screams came closer. If she began singing, they were through.

Tahlia jerked away from Marius. What was she doing?

*Trust me,* she mouthed, holding a finger to her head.

What did that mean?

# CHAPTER 23
## TAHLIA

"Cut yourself!" Lija shouted into Tahlia's ears. "The sea needs your blood."

"What? No time!"

"Come on!" Marius attempted to snatch Tahlia's wrist, and she dodged him, swimming in place an arm's length away.

The siren was swimming toward Tahlia and Marius and although she was bleeding profusely, she was still speeding through the water as quick as a lightning bolt.

"Gods, her skin... She's beautiful. Horrible, but gorgeous and impossible..."

"Rider! Cut! Now!"

Tahlia blinked, pulled her nearest dagger, and sliced the top of her forearm. Blood snaked into the churning water and lightning flashed overhead. Thunder boomed through the ocean.

"She's still coming at us, Lija!"

The siren opened her bloodied mouth to sing.

"Wait," Lija said. "Don't try to out-swim her. She'll just catch you faster. Wait."

"Tahlia!" Marius looked ready to explode.

Tahlia's blood drew into a perfect sphere and pulsed like a heart. "It's doing something, Lija."

The siren's song filtered through the water and Marius began swimming back to his captor.

"Marius! Stop!" The water muffled Tahlia's voice.

"Draw the following rune into the sphere," Lija ordered.

"You know what it looks like?"

Marius stopped swimming toward the siren and pushed back toward Tahlia, rage and shame etched into his features. The siren swam in big circles toward them now, as if she was preparing for a kill like a shark. Her smile was a bracelet of diamonds, her flesh like the sea captured under glass. She was stunning.

"Rider! Focus!" Lija shouted into Tahlia's ears. "Draw a straight, vertical line, then a left to right downward, diagonal slash. Add a crescent on top like a dome and one dot inside the crescent."

Hand shaking, Tahlia did as instructed. Marius stared, his gaze going from her face to the blood and back again. He was frantic and she could almost feel his panic in her chest, thrumming side by side with her fear.

The thunder rolled again, but was it thunder?

Shadows curled from the distant deep blue and from around the coral and rock that shielded the siren's lair.

"What is happening, Lija?"

The dragon's quiet little laugh usually meant someone was about to suffer in exactly the way she wanted them to.

Eels with bright red stripes and jagged teeth shot from the shadows and swam for the siren. Sharks slipped through the water and opened their great maws as they closed in. Where did they come from?

The siren shrieked as she kicked out at a shark's nose. An eel wrapped her wrists and tugged her away from Tahlia and Marius. Another shark bumped her in the back and she whirled, or at least she attempted it, looking more like a broken marionette.

Tahlia set her gaze on Marius, then began to swim toward the surface. He was right beside her in a blink. His eyes said he had numerous questions; hells, so did she.

"Lija, what was that all about? Are you a dragon or maybe a goddess and you've been pretending to be a dragon like the others on the peak?"

Lija chuckled. "Dragons of the sea are more tied to the Unseelie realm than other dragons. We have access to the old magic. Not power enough to best any, but we have tricks hidden between our scales, rider."

"I can see that. I can't wait to hear more about this once we are out of this place."

"Do you know where the crown lies?"

"Not yet, but we are close."

"I wish you all the luck, Lady Tahlia," Lija said. "The communication herb has burned away, so Lady Fara and I will no longer be in contact."

"See you soon."

She walked up the shoreline with the sea tugging once more at her legs. Marius was right beside her. He smoothed his wet Fae-white hair away from his face and squeezed the water from his tangled locks. Drops ran down his inked torso and the muscles of his stomach.

"How are you communicating with Lija?" he asked.

"How did you know?"

"Because that was Seabreak magic," he said, "the likes of which I've only heard about in old stories."

Tahlia twisted her hair and the ends of her tunic, and water splashed onto the stones near her feet. "You've never seen Maiwenn's Donan do anything like that?"

"Similar, but not that powerful. He's never raised an army to defend him from enemies, that's for certain."

Marius wrung the seawater from the loose remains of his ripped trousers while Tahlia put her dry socks and boots back on. Pride in Lija swelled in Tahlia's chest.

"There's an herbwitch at the castle and she helped Fara and Lija communicate with me via my bond with Lija."

"And then talk to me via our mate bond?" Marius found his boots and removed the socks tucked inside.

"Exactly."

Raising his eyebrows, Marius nodded and grunted in approval. Once they were as ready as they could be, he grabbed Tahlia and kissed her hard.

"I'm glad you're still here to ruin my focus, Lady of the Skies."

She nipped his bottom lip and gripped his narrow, delicious, male hips. "Back at you."

They hurried back the way they'd come. The siren's portal remained, shimmering and dizzying. They entered the labyrinth and took a right.

"The minotaur was an illusion. But it was an illusion strong enough to kill," Marius said as they walked on, drawing their blades and shaking or wiping them dry as best they could.

"The siren's doing, I guess?"

"Yes. Did you not feel swayed by her?" Marius asked.

"I did somewhat, but Lija was able to bring me back to myself."

"Thoughts of you are the only reason I was able to strike out at her."

Tahlia's cheeks warmed. "Glad I could help."

The labyrinth went around and around until it reached an arched wooden door with a small, simple brass knob.

"I suppose we're headed in there? The crown is probably sitting right in there on a fine pillow with some magical light illuminating it for us, right?"

Marius lifted one eyebrow and growled.

"Yeah, I didn't think so," she said. "Let's get whatever this nightmare is about to be over with. I'm ready to leave this crazy place."

Marius kicked the door open and Tahlia nearly leapt out of her skin.

"Did the door knob insult you?"

He pushed the broken remnants away and walked forward into the chamber. Tahlia followed him. The room was a twenty-by-thirty-foot dusty enclosure. Footprints ran in a crescent shape around a raised platform crafted of dark wood. On top, a box large enough for three crowns boasted a seashell-shaped lock.

"That has to be it, right?" Tahlia asked. "Or is this another ruse?"

"We won't know unless we try it. Can you still

communicate with Lija? She may know something about such a lock."

"Because of its shape."

"Aye."

"I can't talk to her anymore, I don't think. She said the herbwitch ran out of the rare plant that allowed us that link. I'll try though just in case."

Marius nodded, and from the small bag at his belt, he removed the key the contact had given them at the warehouse.

"Lija? Fara? Can you hear me?" Tahlia closed her eyes to focus, listening for any sound, any whisper.

Sighing, she opened her eyes and shook her head. "No go."

Marius jerked his chin in understanding. "Tell me immediately if you notice anything amiss when I put the key in place."

"Do you think that's the right key?"

Chewing his lip, Marius lifted his eyebrows. "There's a solid chance it is. That contact has worked in Spycraft since he was a child. It's in his family."

"You know them?" Tahlia asked.

"I've heard of them."

Glancing around the room once more, he lifted the key to the seashell lock. His shoulders moved in a breath and he inserted the key. The lock clicked, the sound loud in the small and silent chamber. The walls had to be incredibly thick because not even the sea's crashing was audible here. The seashell fell open and the corner of Marius's lips tilted up in a half grin. He removed the lock and Tahlia took it from him, tucking it into her pocket. He lifted the box's lid…

Another box sat inside with another lock, this one in the shape of a fist.

"Think the little key will help us one more time?" Tahlia removed it from her pocket and stuck it into the fist. "It fits!" She tried to turn it, but the lock didn't give. "Damn. I was hoping it would be that easy."

"Easy?" Marius stared at her, wide-eyed. "A collapsing floor, a bespelled darkness, a minotaur, and a siren, and you call that *easy*?"

"We made our way through it all, didn't we? I only have some sore ribs and an angry ankle."

"Maybe you have a terrible concussion. I don't think you're clearheaded at the moment."

Tahlia grinned and smacked his arm. "Shut it, you big lug."

Marius pursed his lips and lifted the box carefully. "Maybe it's time for a blunt approach."

He slammed the box onto the floor. Tahlia gasped as the wood splintered as the door had. There was nothing inside the box. But then again, the crown was invisible.

Marius took the concoction the Witch had given them from his pouch, uncorked it, and sprinkled the floral-scented blend over the mess of what had been the second box. The air glimmered as if it was under water with the sun shining on ripples of seawater.

"Is it not working or is the crown not in here?" Tahlia fisted her hands.

Durniad would be here soon, if their information was accurate. Sweat beaded on her upper lip and she swallowed while Marius bent to squint at the sparkling area.

"Look." He pointed near a broken corner of the box.

Fingers of a dark metal appeared out of the Witch's shimmering magic. The tines came together with sapphire circles and bronze leaves, and soon, the crown showed itself in full.

"Can you just pick it up?" Tahlia asked. "Is the crown's power only activated if you put it on?"

Marius exhaled. "That's what King Lysanael said."

A shuffling sounded behind them. "Is that so?"

Tahlia's heart iced over.

Durniad.

CHAPTER 24

# MARIUS

As fast as he could, Marius set the crown on his own head and got between Tahlia and Durniad. Magic shivered down his back and along his jaw. The cooling sensation traveled along his throat and into his chest.

Durniad's smug look had fallen and his eyes looked ready to pop from his meaty head.

"You see the one who should wear the crown wearing it now," Marius said, not knowing what in the hells he was doing, but desperate to escape with Tahlia. He had been ordered to avoid bloodshed if possible. But with Durniad flanked by four large guards, the crown was the only way they could leave without a great deal of damage and a high body count.

Tahlia's hand found Marius's back, and he was glad he wore no tunic because he could easily feel that her fingers didn't shake. She wasn't afraid of the power he held at the moment. His mate truly trusted him.

Durniad blinked quickly, then he and his guards stepped aside.

Marius started down the labyrinth with Tahlia behind him.

"This is great!" Tahlia whispered. "Oooh, tell me to do something. I want to see how it feels."

"This isn't a game, Lady Tahlia."

"Aw, come on, Commander. Make me run or say the alphabet backwards."

"Your ankle is injured."

"Actually, it's good now. My ribs and head aren't great, but I'm fine. Do the alphabet one. Wait. I know I'm not capable of that. What if I explode when you order me to try?"

"You are far too excited about the prospect."

"It's fascinating!"

"Spontaneous combustion would compromise our mission."

"You're so Marius, you know that?"

He frowned. "Why would I be anything else?"

A shrieking shattered Marius's thoughts.

They whirled to see the siren dragging herself through her portal behind them.

Tahlia swore in a Fara-like manner—some curse involving monkeys and testes. Marius agreed with the sentiment if not the communication style.

The siren had lost an arm. Her watery flesh had gone blood red. She looked like a true nightmare now, her jeweled eyes gone cloudy and her mouth ripped at one side.

"I will have my revenge." She rushed them—moving faster than anything Marius had ever witnessed—and snatched Tahlia's belt.

Marius's body went tight with battle readiness. The siren wavered on her feet. The surge of activity had depleted her somewhat. She was weakened.

The siren hauled Tahlia backward, the creature's arm laced around Tahlia's neck. Opening her mouth of coral and shark teeth, the siren prepared to bite down on Tahlia's shoulder. Panic threaded through Marius's every bone, tendon, and muscle.

"Get off me!" Tahlia snarled, grabbed the siren's arm, maneuvered her hips, and slammed the siren onto the floor. "Ugh. Your skin feels so bizarre." She shook water from her hands and grimaced.

The creature howled and slowly raised herself back up.

Tahlia drew her two daggers and slashed at the siren's gut, but the creature evaded her and hissed.

"Leave. Go back to the sea," Marius demanded.

"That crown has no power over me," the siren whispered.

Her power must have been diminished by her injuries because her voice didn't seem to affect Tahlia or him at all.

The siren lashed out with her fingers. Each watery digit ended with a claw made of some dark coral that leaked a foul, green substance that would poison Tahlia if she made contact. Marius knew that some-how. The scent of the stuff made the hairs on the back of his neck rise.

A rushing sounded. Tahlia glanced at him, keeping a blade between her and the siren.

What was that sound?

The siren's arm became a small torrent of rushing water, and the siren encircled Tahlia's neck, choking her and pulling her close.

"Stop!" Marius lunged forward with his dagger outstretched, but he couldn't do anything without further threatening Tahlia's safety.

Tahlia was choking, her eyes panicked and her cheeks red. A shout sounded behind the siren and Tahlia. Durniad tore Tahlia from the injured siren's arms.

"Get me that crown, siren, and you get your revenge," Durniad said.

"You want to release her," Marius ordered. The crown's power shivered down his spine and throat.

Gaze going blank, Durniad did so, but the siren's entire body turned into a rushing wave and drove

Marius to the ground. He leapt up again, but the crown was gone from his drenched head.

The siren reformed. Tahlia slashed the siren's waist. Water gushed from the wound. The creature hissed and snared Tahlia's hair. Shouting in pain, Tahlia dropped her blade. The siren yanked Tahlia out of Marius's reach. He froze. The siren's abilities were an unknown. He had to stall and figure this out. Tahlia's face said she too was trying to work out a strategy here.

"Why are you working with him?" Marius asked the siren, truly baffled.

"His great-grandsire killed my mother's enemy. My mother created that crown and I owe him a blood debt."

Damn. Marius couldn't twist that to their benefit.

With a cocky laugh, Durniad placed the crown on his head. "Drop all your weapons," he ordered Marius.

To keep up their ruse that they were human, Marius dropped his daggers while the siren dragged Tahlia toward the portal. Marius could not, would not, permit the siren to take her. His body hummed with rage.

"Take me," Tahlia said, her tone casual. "I'll call up my ocean pals to rip your face off the second we hit the water."

"Not if I bind your hands so you can't make runes," the siren said.

Tahlia laughed. "That's what you think. I'm not the creature you think I am."

The warped grin on the siren's injured face fell, and Durniad frowned, his brow furrowing with confusion.

A tingling zipped along Marius's ears, jaw, and down his whole body. He watched as Tahlia's ears grew back into their regular pointed shape and her irises returned to their slitted, Fae form. He touched his ear, and yes, the Witch's potion had reached the end of its time limit.

The siren hissed and shoved Tahlia to the ground. Her cheek hit the ground hard and she groaned, immediately trying to pull herself back up.

"Stay on the ground, woman," Durniad said, not realizing she was part Fae. Would the amount of Fae blood she had be enough?

The siren fled through her portal. The shimmering opening fizzled like water on a hot stone and then it disappeared entirely.

"I don't know what your backstory is with the siren," Durniad said, "but I don't care. I think I'm ready for some entertainment. My grand plan takes off very soon, so I don't have all day."

Tahlia glanced at Marius and remained on the ground as if the crown did hold sway over her body. Was she faking like him?

Marius was a living storm of indecision. Durniad

hadn't yet noticed Marius's ears and eyes. Should he attack Durniad and his men in hopes of grabbing the crown and releasing Tahlia? Or should he keep still in case Durniad truly did control Tahlia? The makeshift king could order her to ram her own head into the wall and end herself.

Swallowing the bitter taste of fear on the back of his tongue, Marius stared at Tahlia. He hoped for a wink only he would see or some other indication. But Tahlia remained still. Her gaze stayed on him, but her look told him absolutely nothing.

"King Durniad!" one of the human's guards rushed toward Tahlia.

Marius started toward him, fuming.

"Stay," Durniad ordered.

Marius held himself back as the guard moved Tahlia's hair away from her ear.

"What is it?" Durniad spat as he studied Marius with a look that said he was deciding how to torture him.

"Her ears. She's Fae." The guard lifted his head and eyed Marius. "Him too."

Durniad stepped forward, getting closer to Tahlia, who lay between him and Marius. "Hmm. Now why would the Fae be involved here? And how is my crown controlling them if their blood isn't human?" His delighted grin made Marius's skin crawl. "Perhaps I should rework my grand plan and make it even grander."

He set his foot on Tahlia's lower back and she grunted, likely her ribs paining her. Gods, Marius was going to kill Durniad very, very slowly when the right moment came. He savored the thought of it.

"Maybe they're half-breeds like Syonia," the guard said.

"Ah." Durniad clicked his tongue. "That would explain it. Let's test this out, shall we?"

Marius growled.

"Oooh, you are protective of her. She is your friend? No, I think she is more than that. Don't Fae mate for life?"

"They mate casually, but they mate in another way for life," the guard said, his distaste for Fae apparent in his sneer.

The feeling was mutual. Marius felt another growl building in the back of his throat.

"That's what my Veilbury cousin told me anyway," the guard said.

Durniad nodded at his knowledgeable guard. He removed his foot from Tahlia's back. "Stand, half-breed."

She did so with odd, jerky movements. So she was actually controlled by Durniad. The magic of the crown obviously wasn't as overpowering on her as it was on the full-blooded humans. Marius weighed his ideas and how that could help them. He had to get her out of here before Durniad did something truly terrible. Marius knew he could take the guards and Durniad, but while Durniad had the crown, Tahlia was in serious danger. He didn't dare attack. Not yet anyway.

*Ragewing, if there is any way you can hear me, please let me know. We are in a tight spot and I might have to throw caution to the wind and ask you to charge in for a rescue.*

There was no response. Damn the distance between them.

What could he do? Marius ground his teeth and bared his fangs. Durniad glanced his way and paled slightly as he adjusted his crown.

"Easy now," Durniad said to Marius. "Don't go feral on me." He faced Tahlia.

Marius could only think to stall the madman, to give himself some time to come up with a plan.

"King Durniad," Marius said, "why do you want this crown? Why this elaborate protection? What do you want of life?"

"Such big questions from an intruder. Listen, no one else has the stones to take what we, the people of Midhampton, need. We were the first human city to have art and high-level architecture on the continent. The first to begin trade with the east and north. We deserve to thrive and use this gift Fate has set in our laps. I do this for my people." He fisted his hand and pounded it once against his barrel-like chest. "I was born to be their king and to bring them back to the top of the world. There will be no starving in our streets. No mistreated children or people worked to death. We will be as fat as pigs and as wealthy as our kings of old. We will be the center of civilization again and all will come to us for advice and to raise their level of living."

"No one could fault you for lack of confidence," Tahlia muttered.

"Do not speak, either of you. Unless I demand it."

Marius acted at not being able to say another word, opening his mouth and pretending no sound would come.

Durniad eyed Tahlia with a detached look. "Break one of your fingers," he commanded.

Marius's stomach dropped. His entire mind focused on murder. He would bleed this man dry.

Tahlia's lips pressed tightly together. She gripped her left pinkie finger and Marius held his breath.

# CHAPTER 25

# TAHLIA

The urge to follow the madman's command was like a terrible itch under Tahlia's skin. She set her jaw, refusing the crown's demand, pushing it away like her thoughts were giant palms in sand made of magic. *I am Tahlia. I will not go down like this. I refuse anyone else's will being imposed on me. I have my own mind and I will use it.* She chanted that inside her head. The magic shivered over her, but its influence weakened. She released her finger and glared at Durniad.

With a shout of pent-up rage, Marius launched himself at Durniad. He drove a fist into his throat. The crown went flying and freed Tahlia's body. She spun and hit the nearest guard with an elbow to the temple. Drawing her dagger, she watched Marius snag one of his blades from the floor in a blur of incredible speed. They cut the guards down, but Durniad rose behind them. He went for the crown that had skidded across the floor. He placed it on himself.

"Guards!" he called over the labyrinth. "Kill my enemies!"

A rush of boots sounded at the beginning of the labyrinth and soon guards were pouring into the walled space. Their eyes were glazed and their movements frantic as they came with swords, fists, and even objects that were never meant to serve as weapons—a set of manacles, what appeared to be a hair comb from one man's pocket, and a scroll one fellow brandished like a knife.

The guard who had helped Tahlia and Marius earlier swung a book at Tahlia. She ducked, set her head on the woman's hip, and grabbed the backs of the woman's knees. The guard went down with a grunt.

They couldn't maintain this level of fighting. The walls beckoned.

Tahlia kicked a man's stomach, throwing him back. She jumped off the back of a staggering, mostly collapsed guard whom Marius had hit and leapt onto the top of the labyrinth's walls.

"Up here!" she called down to Marius.

He bent his knees and jumped up beside her, and

then they were running, dodging arrows, and leaping over sloppily tossed daggers.

The doorway into the chamber was empty. All the occupants within hearing range of the crown's influence must have already entered the labyrinth.

"What's our plan?" Tahlia asked as they jumped down and fled the chamber.

"Run like those cakes you love are at the end!"

Tahlia cackled as they swept up the stairs and ran out the side door of the fortress. There weren't any guards anywhere. The larger street they came out on was still flowing red with tomatoes, and people were dancing and playing pipes and lutes everywhere. Mugs were lifted and toasts shouted as Tahlia and Marius wove through the mess of humanity.

"We Fae should take a page from their books," Tahlia said loudly as they came to a meat pie cart that had been overturned in the ruckus.

Marius grabbed her wrist and turned them down an alleyway that headed roughly toward the city gates.

"I'm serious," she said, glancing at his scowling face. "They aren't worried about appearances. Only fun, fun, and more fun. Our kind could use some more of that."

She didn't feel odd saying our kind because she had been raised in the Realm of Lights as a Fae and had always considered herself Fae even though she was half. But looking around at the humans, she realized this was what she'd been missing. This pure and simple embracing of joy. This was part of what it meant to have human blood.

"Less talking. More running, Tahlia."

A now familiar voice carried on the wind, the words strung out as if shouted from afar.

"People of Midhampton, stop the white-haired Fae male and small half-Fae female if you see them. Use whatever means necessary to bring them alive to me."

The command held no spark of magic that Tahlia could feel, but that was likely only because Durniad hadn't directed the order at her. Or was it because she had fought the magic earlier and managed to break its hold?

"How does he know you are full Fae and I'm half?" she asked.

"I moved easily against him," Marius said. "Your movements were clearly hindered. I'm thinking he is simply very good at making judgment calls."

Marius led her to the edge of the main street with Bodwin Bridge in the near distance. The entire mass of humans dropped their hands to their sides and their smiles fell into flat looks of magical obedience.

They started toward Tahlia and Marius.

"Well, this is just fantastic. What's our new plan? Because running for cakes seems a tiny bit completely impossible at the moment."

They backed up as three men and a woman neared them, one with a pipe extended like a blade and the other two with hands outstretched.

Grimacing, Tahlia moved back another step and glanced over her shoulder, probably to check for more humans approaching. Thankfully, that side was clear.

"This would honestly be hilarious if they weren't trying to beat us up and hand us to an all-powerful madman," she whispered.

Marius grunted, his gaze darting to the buildings surrounding them. "Let's climb."

"Don't have to tell me twice." Tahlia grabbed the closest downspout and began scrambling up the side of a tailor's shop.

Using his full Fae strength and agility, Marius jumped onto a low balcony, then reached up to swing onto a second balcony above that one. Soon, they were both on the roof, looking down at the nightmare this day had become.

The people of the city lifted their heads as one to watch Marius and Tahlia. Durniad stood on one of the many temporary wooden stages the city had erected for the festival. The crown shimmered on his brow and he lifted a bronze speaking tube to his lips.

"Climb, you idiots!" Durniad shouted. "Shoot arrows at them if you can. Just don't kill them. Not yet!"

"Can they do that? I mean, with half-human

blood, I can't do what you did on those balconies. They are fully human; surely they can't scale this..."

Her words faded from her tongue as a slender brown-haired human man began to climb the building next to the one they were on. He used the jutting spots of plaster and planks of wood support to rise higher and higher. Slowly but surely, more followed the man. They would be overrun in a matter of minutes.

"Marius. Listen. I broke the crown's hold on my mind by reminding myself who I was. I pushed the urge to obey the crown away. Maybe I can help everyone do that too?"

"They're human. You have Fae blood. You were able to do that because of your Fae blood."

"I don't think so. I think it was my human blood fighting something that threatened its freedom. Humans enjoy doing exactly what they want to do."

"And Fae don't?"

"Fae are more instinctive. Don't you agree?"

Marius tipped his head to one side and shrugged. The movement meant he saw her point but didn't love it.

"I'm going to talk to them." She stepped even closer to the front edge of the building.

Marius was right beside her. "They will be here in a moment. We must figure out a way across to the building behind us. Just there. Then perhaps we can find a way to the city wall and down."

"And maybe I'll sprout wings. Come on, Marius. We are completely toasted here. No chance unless I make this work."

"Tahlia."

Tahlia paused, the tone in his voice tugging at her heart. "What's really wrong? You're acting off." She spoke quickly. They were about to be overrun with attackers, so there really wasn't time for this, but... "Something is bothering you. I mean, aside from all this." Waving her hand around, she indicated their current situation.

"You don't realize how simultaneously weak and evil humans are."

That actually hurt a bit. "I think I do. I am half one of them."

He shook his head like there was a bee in his ear. "You're not truly, though. When they killed Bellona..." His throat moved and his eyes shuttered briefly.

Her chest went tight and she gripped his forearm. "Oh." She finally understood what he'd been dealing with during this mission. "Marius, you know, deep down, that the humans are good and bad and everything in between. Just as the Fae are. We are all faulty and kind and cruel and beautiful. We are all complicated creatures."

He exhaled roughly, his gaze going to the ledge. "We can talk more when we aren't in mortal danger."

"Agreed." Not waiting for him to say more, she

lifted her arms. "Hello, humans! I am half-human and I've enjoyed watching you embrace life in all its messy glory. Break the hold Durniad has on you by reminding yourself that you are you and you have the freedom to do exactly as you see fit. Find your center. Imagine pushing Durniad's magical influence away from you."

A few here and there blinked and frowned as if they were hearing her, but not quite understanding. She repeated her words.

"No tyrant will control us! No tyrant will control us!" She shouted the phrase again and again and soon the festival-drunk crowd was echoing her, joining in on the chant, their faces clearing of enchantment and showing anger as they turned to face Durniad.

Marius stood beside Tahlia, his mouth parted in shock.

Tahlia squeezed his hand. "They are not the villains here. They are victims."

Nodding, Marius stared and stared.

Durniad shouted at his guards.

Tahlia squinted at a shape some guards appeared to be pulling from a space between two buildings. "What is that?"

Carted on two large wheels, the contraption had wooden arms and a complicated system of ropes.

"I'm not sure, but that is definitely a giant crossbow bolt," Marius said.

"Aw, is that for us? Durniad, the gift giver."

"I doubt it's for us, actually." Marius turned and looked into the cloudy sky.

As Tahlia lifted her face, a thrilling blend of hope and fear shot through her veins.

# CHAPTER 26

# MARIUS

A scarlet shape too high and far away for Marius to see clearly plunged from the cloud cover.

"Ragewing!" Both he and Tahlia shouted the dragon's name as he flew toward them.

*You called,* the dragon said inside Marius's mind. He tucked his wings and began to dive.

*I didn't realize you could hear me. Watch out for the ballista. I've heard they can launch a bolt higher than a three-story building.* Marius hated that he was about to witness the firing of a weapon the order had only talked about in wary whispers.

*Ready yourselves,* Ragewing said. *I'll fly low between the building you're on and the blacksmith's forge.*

Behind them. *All right.*

*Try to get onto my back so I can tuck in my legs.*

*We will.*

It made more sense because *en talon* transportation would be a nightmare with flying projectiles coming from the ground.

Tahlia didn't ask questions; she followed Marius as he ran over one of the roof's shingled peaks and toward the back of the building.

The ballista had Marius wondering if Durniad had known all along that the Mist Knights were working with the human high queen against him, or at the very least, had realized the possibility. Sure, the ballistas were good for fighting encroaching ships in the harbor, but on this side of the city, the weapons were only truly good for taking down dragons.

Below, the humans were still fighting the crown's power. A terrible sound rose over the murmurs and shouts of the crowd. The sound was like the twang of a bow but so much louder.

Ragewing spread his wings slightly and angled himself to fly along the edge of the buildings down the back street. A bolt the size of a small tree shot through the air and narrowly missed the tip of Ragewing's right wing.

"Watch out!" Tahlia cried.

The dragon roared and people screamed, running like rodents along the street below. Not rodents, Marius corrected himself. Humans. Good ones who were like Tahlia and Queen Revna.

Ragewing zipped toward them.

"Now!" Marius's heart climbed up his throat.

He and Tahlia jumped onto the dragon's moving back.

Tahlia sat behind Marius, her voice in his ear. "We can't leave yet, can we? Try to lie, I beg you."

Ragewing's scales were hot. He had been flying hard or he was stressed or both.

"We have to get the crown," Marius yelled toward Ragewing's ears.

"Damn all-powerful artifacts. Always ruining our day," Tahlia said, the wind snatching at her words.

Marius slid a bit because Ragewing wore no saddle. He still had part of his reins on—a leather strap that reached across his back and joined under his front legs. Marius grabbed hold of the strap. Flying higher, Ragewing left the cover of the buildings and rushed toward Durniad.

And straight toward the ballista.

Tahlia laced her arms more tightly around Marius's waist. "I hope they take another ten minutes to reload that evil contraption."

Men were pulling at the ballista's twisted ropes while Durniad commanded them to hurry.

"Hold on to his spikes now, Lady Tahlia," Marius said, allowing his training to kick in and drive his worry away. He became the cold warrior, the Shadow of the Shrouded Mountains. "You're not struggling against the crown's power, are you? I don't want you leaping from Ragewing's back when I least expect it."

"I've conquered it. I can feel its influence, but I can fight it pretty easily now."

"I love knowing that."

He edged his way down Ragewing's side, keeping one hand on the strap and dropping his other arm low to ready himself.

"You're going to lift it right off his head?" Tahlia asked, laughter in her voice.

Gods, she was fearless sometimes. "Aye." He longed to ask Ragewing to lift the man and drop him from the clouds, but killing Durniad wasn't part of the mission unfortunately and they'd already broken enough of the rules to get themselves into a load of trouble.

Ragewing flew low. The men tipped the ballista and readied to fire. Durniad's face purpled as he shouted to his men.

A wicked grin tugged at Marius's lips. He leaned low on Ragewing's side, then swiped the crown.

"Be glad I let you keep your head, Durniad!" he shouted.

Ragewing sped sharply toward the open sky, climbing so quickly that Marius's breath caught. The twang of the ballista sounded.

Ragewing shrieked. The scent of dragon's blood

filled Marius's nose and they began to tumble downward.

*I lost her!* Ragewing shouted into Marius's mind.

The city's structures sped closer and closer.

*What?* Marius whirled and his body went rigid.

Tahlia had disappeared. Blood flowed from Ragewing's tail.

# CHAPTER 27
# TAHLIA

Tahlia slipped through the sky end over end. Her view of Ragewing and Marius blurred, but the blood flecking out from the top side of Ragewing's tail was unmistakable. The bolt wasn't visible, but it had surely been the cause.

She hit the water hard. Cold enveloped her, but she couldn't be mad. At least it was water instead of cobblestone or one of Bodwin Bridge's spikey torch posts. Lungs burning, she swam toward the surface. She broke through at last, gasped, and looked up to check on Ragewing and Marius. They were no longer tumbling, and they had flown toward the city gates.

"Get her," Durniad commanded from the bank side.

His guards did as ordered, splashing into the drink

after her, but the people of Midhampton were less than thrilled with the day's events.

The crowd shouted at Durniad.

"You tricked us!"

"We won't be shoved about with dark magic!"

Some were simply confused.

"What is going on?"

"Was that really a dragon or part of the magic?"

"Are you Unseelie, Durniad? Are you Fae?"

"Someone bring him down here to explain himself!"

Flustered, Durniad ignored the yelling and focused on Tahlia. She couldn't exactly remain in the water and no doubt Ragewing had to leave the city and find someone to patch him up. So she thought she might as well go along with the guards.

She swam over to them. "Fine. You have me. But be aware, fellas. The big red boy up there isn't the only dragon I know. And I'm pretty sure Big Red will return fairly soon and he will be powerfully angry."

The guards grabbed her under the arms and hauled her out of the slanted riverside. To their credit, though they paled at her warning, they held her tightly and didn't make a sound to give away their fear.

"Listen, I'm half-human. I am a lot like you. You can see this Durniad arsehead is a complete wreck of a person, right? Why follow him? The crowd is behind us. Let's overthrow him right now. It'll be fun!"

"Shut it, woman," the guard on her right snapped.

"Don't act like you're not thinking about it," she whispered as they dragged her toward their fool of a boss.

Durniad's dark blond hair stuck to his sweating forehead. He pointed at Tahlia with a thick forefinger. "I have a delightful surprise for you, my dear."

"I seriously doubt my reaction is going to match your expectations."

"No, you don't understand."

"I don't comprehend you? I agree."

The madman chuckled and came close. Tahlia could break out of these guards' sad little hold on her arms, but it would be smarter to wait for a better moment to escape. Granted, said adventure would need to happen before they locked her into a dungeon somewhere or lopped off her head or whatever sick stuff Durniad had planned for her.

"I am going to make you my queen."

Tahlia's mouth fell open. She nodded slowly and exhaled. "I have news that's going to disappoint you, good sir."

He frowned, then one of the guards holding Tahlia said,"She's mated to that Fae male on the dragon, my king."

Durniad waved off the man's words like they were

annoying gnats. "We aren't in the Realm of Lights now, are we? We are in the human world. I can be her human husband. We will wash that Fae side right out of her."

"Why in the name of all the gods would you want to wed me? I loathe you. And let's get really honest here. I could kill you. Pretty easily."

A laugh boomed from Durniad as they started down the steps of the festival stage. Durniad must have ordered more guards into the streets because the crowd was breaking up now under the strike of clubs, swords, and fists.

"You entertain me, lady. Now, what is your name?"

"Why don't you call me whatever you like since you seem to think you're a god."

"I am rather like one, aren't I? Fully in control of my fate despite setbacks. I am unbeatable even without the crown."

"Are you though? Because my mate isn't finished with this fight. I can promise you that."

He chuckled again—a disgusting sound that included a sort of wheeze—and led his men forward. Tahlia didn't tug at her captors, but instead, she let them carry her along, giving herself some rest. She'd be slipping away shortly and she needed the energy to run and climb.

"Well, if I am going to be your sweetheart, maybe you could give me some food? I'm starving."

"Of course!" Durniad smiled at her over his thick shoulder. "You'll have everything you want. You'll be a queen. We will reign here on the off-seasons."

"Off-seasons of what?"

He lifted a hand. His sleeve fell back and a pirate's inking showed—this particular rendition being a skull and a sword. "Pirating, of course."

"Ah, yes. I forgot you don't restrict your arseholery to land-based situations."

"Such a naughty tongue."

"Please don't make a disgusting joke. That's such a droll, villain thing to do. Be more creative."

The madman's shoulders shook as he laughed. "I'll have to sharpen my wit for you, my dearest."

"Well, listen. This has been fun, but I have things to do and places to be."

Tahlia dropped her weight. The guards grunted and their holds on her arms loosened. She slammed her elbow into one guard's groin and spun to knee the other's stones. Whirling, she lunged away from them and the three who had been walking behind them. She smashed into the smaller of the three, sending him into the taller two, and then she was running.

Down the road. Through the guards beating the hells out of the crowd. Around a cluster of angry men and women brandishing kitchen cutlery at Durniad's men.

"Keep that up!" she shouted, trying to encourage

them. "I'll come back with a dragon or two and help you out!"

They cheered her as she climbed a downspout and headed for the rooftops. The sun blazed onto her head as she jumped from building to building. Shouting erupted from the streets she leapt over. More guards. The city walls were only three roofs away. She could do this. She'd climb down the walls, fight whom she had to, then run into the forest and find Marius and Ragewing. Unless they found her first, which would be even better because that would mean Ragewing was patched up enough to fly them to the Witch's house to deliver the crown and end this wild mission.

With the last big jump, Tahlia landed on the city's three-Fae-wide protective wall. She smiled, hope making her feel like she could best ten of these guards with one hand tied behind her back.

Twisting, she fell from the wall and darkness swept over her before she could see what had struck her.

# CHAPTER 28

# MARIUS

Ragewing growled as Marius knotted up the sad excuse for a bandage on the top of the dragon's wound. He'd been forced to use the bottom half of his trousers and part of the leather strap that usually stretched over Ragewing's shoulders as an additional part of his rein system.

*Not so tight,* Ragewing hissed inside Marius's head.

*It must be so you can fly back and not risk bleeding out.*

*Rider, I can't fly into Midhampton to rescue Lady Tahlia and you know it. As much as I wish I could, they will have me down and we will only end up giving them more captives.*

*We must. I'm sorry, but we must. They'll kill her.* Marius's entire body hummed with pent-up violence. It was unthinkable what that madman might be doing to her. If she'd even survived the fall. No, he couldn't imagine she wasn't alive. If he did, he'd go as mad as Durniad.

*They won't.*

*You don't know that.*

*She's a valued member of the Fae realm. Durniad knows not to risk angering King Lysanael and Queen Revna.*

*Does he? Because he spends his autumns ravaging the northern coast. His pirate crews have led attacks that we have fought against, Ragewing. He is not cowed by anything even if it would be wise to back down.*

*This is different. He is greedy. We know that. He will want to use Lady Tahlia's life to get something from the king and queen. And perhaps from his human high queen as well, if he can work an angle that makes sense.*

Marius fisted his hands so tightly that his knuckles cracked.

*You'll break a fang if you grit your teeth like that.*

Glaring at the dragon, Marius battled the impotent rage storming inside his heart and soul and mind.

*Breathe, rider. Breathe and think. Be cold. Store the anger for later and plot. You can do this. I'm with you.*

His mind whirled, panic lancing through his thought processes, jumbling potential plans with random imaginings of ripping Durniad's head from his body. He closed his eyes and set a hand on Ragewing. The dragon's side moved steadily in and out as he breathed, and Marius matched the rhythm, inhaling and exhaling slowly.

*What do we have to use?* Ragewing's question was quiet and calm. *Materials. Allies. Environment.*

*The crown. Two blades at my belt. Our main contact is likely stuck in the city, but perhaps he'll be able to do something to help Lady Tahlia. We have your fire if we can get you into the air for at least a little while. The Witch isn't too far for me to reach on foot if you must rest.*

*I can fly to the Witch's house. Will she help us?* Ragewing shuffled his wings and adjusted the lay of his tail, wincing and flashing vicious white teeth.

*I would think so. This is her queen's mission, after all.*

*But we have the crown already. Will she care that we left a knight behind?*

*She doesn't have to know we have the crown,* Marius said. *The crown's power worked in two ways from what I saw in the city. If a human is within earshot, they can be heavily influenced. And the influence seems to spread like an illness, catching from one to the next.*

*The magic most likely manipulates a person's energy, then,* Ragewing said.

*I'm not sure I fully understand any of its magic.*

Ragewing let out a plume of fire smoke, which he often did when thinking. *Me neither.*

*Let's say I enter the city again using the crown to control the humans as I go,* Marius said.

Ragewing's body was very warm, as if he was

ready to breathe fire. *Will it matter if they stop up their ears? Because I would assume Durniad will be giving orders to do that if it blocks the crown's influence.*

Marius nodded. *I think that would keep the crown's magic from working except in those cases when it already has a human under its control and that human nears the one with stopped-up ears. The virus, so to speak, of the crown's control would spread regardless.*

*So stealth would be in order. Durniad could hurt Lady Tahlia if he sees you coming.*

Yes, Marius said, *We would have to attempt to sneak in again without being recognized...*

Ragewing grunted and shifted his weight, adjusting the way he rested on the ground. *But you don't have any more of the Witch's potion to disguise yourself.*

*No. Let's visit her and see if she will help us once more. We'll pretend we don't have the crown.*

*Perhaps you should hide the crown here somewhere,* Ragewing said, *so you can deceive her more easily since you truly won't have the crown in hand.*

*Good idea. But I think I'll simply hide it outside the Witch's house. I don't like the thought of leaving this powerful artifact unguarded here in the woods.*

He unbuckled his belt, slipped the leather through the artifact, then put the belt back on, securing the crown to himself. He could remove it upon arrival and hide it in the greenery near the Witch's abode.

# CHAPTER 29
## TAHLIA

Tahlia opened her eyes for the third time since she'd fallen from the city wall. This time she was less dead so she actually felt the injury in her side.

"Ugh. Kill me."

The room was bright because the evil sun was shining through a high window. A bandage wrapped around her torso, a bit of blood staining the linen.

A female human approached the cot she was resting on. "Never saw someone with Fae blood heal in front of my eyes. Amazing."

"Glad to entertain. Why don't you stab me with another little something and we can both enjoy the power of magic all over again?"

"Oooh, would you be willing?"

"Kidding, woman. I was kidding."

She bit her lip and had the grace to look ashamed. Gods, Tahlia wouldn't be able to murder her in order to escape. She was too sweet.

"Is Durniad around? Where exactly am I? What happened?"

"You were shot with an arrow. It didn't pierce anything important."

"I count skin as important."

"Ah." She shook her head like Tahlia was silly. "King Durniad will be here shortly. You're in his fortress."

"The same place where he stashed that horrible crown and tried to kill me the first time?"

"Probably, yes, although I wasn't privy to all of that business," she said chirpily.

Tahlia shut her eyes. She definitely hadn't healed fully in front of this woman's eyes because with every heartbeat, pain lashed at her side.

"Tons of guards outside, huh?" Tahlia asked, hoping to tease some information from the Healer.

"Of course. The king wants you to stay put on account of your upcoming nuptials."

"You think I should marry him?"

The Healer glanced at the closed door and grimaced. "No. I do not."

Tahlia snorted. "Great. Then can you help me escape?"

"I wish. But I just landed this job. I used to be a tanner's wife."

"You left him?"

She grinned widely. "He died."

Tahlia laughed. "I guess he deserves that vicious joy on your face?"

"Completely."

"You remind me of my friend, Fara. She's a Healer too. Maybe a person has to be vicious to sew folks up all day."

"You do, yes. Or you'd be weeping or puking or both during every shift."

Tahlia nodded. "Now, about that escape..."

"I could look away maybe while you check out the window up there..." The Healer raised her pale eyebrows.

Tahlia twisted, wincing, and eyed the window in question. "It's forty feet up with nothing to climb to get there."

"But you're half-Fae."

"I hate to burst your bubble, but we can't leap that high. At least, I can't."

"Too bad your dragon isn't here. I heard you're a Mist Knight of the Shrouded Mountains."

Of course she knew who they were. Ragewing had completed their already-pretty-much-blown cover situation. King Lysanael was not going to be best pleased. But Tahlia wasn't going to worry about any of that until she got out of here still breathing.

"What about that door there?" Tahlia jerked her chin at a slender wooden door in the corner of the room.

"That's a privy."

"Perfect." It would dump into a body of water, hopefully.

The Healer helped her up and walked her to the door. "I'll leave you to it unless you call out, all right?"

Nodding, Tahlia entered the privy. This wasn't going to be fun.

"I hope the humans and Fae alike appreciate my sacrifice here."

They had managed to take the crown from Durniad. The mission was at least successful in that regard. Marius would try to come back for her. She had no doubt about that, but would he have any support? They'd already created a fantastic mess and sending someone back in would only make more waves. The human high queen and her regent didn't want this snatch-and-grab job to point to them at all. So perhaps it would make sense to return and rescue her so Durniad wouldn't have her to question?

Well, Tahlia wasn't waiting on Marius. She was leaving. Now.

Even if she had to deal with a privy.

She lifted the wooden seat and squinted through

the hole carved into the stone floor. Several stories down, a narrow river ran quickly along the fortress's base, no doubt heading for the sea. She blew out a breath. Could she fit through that hole? Would she break her body further if she landed wrong? Lots of questions. No answers. And she wouldn't figure it out mulling about in here.

Wishing she had her boots and bemoaning the fact that they'd stripped her of her weapons belt, she sat backwards on the privy's seat, held her feet together, then launched herself down, down, down.

The carved hole out of the fortress hit her spine as she fell awkwardly. Pain shook her and she tried to straighten her legs again, working her position so she'd land feet first in the water.

The river's embrace wasn't for the faint of heart. The cold and the strike of the surface made her cry out in agony, her side flaring with pain and her back shrieking with what was going to be a mighty bruise. Carrying her past the fortress, the river gurgled around her ears. She spread her arms wide to keep her head above water.

She could practically hear Fara's voice in her head.

*Can't believe you jumped into a privy and the refuse river with a hole in your side? And how many times have you fallen through the air today alone? You truly do want to perish horribly, don't you?*

Tahlia's thoughts tumbled along with the river,

her cheeks flushing though her body was cold from the water. She hoped she wouldn't be suddenly dumped into the sea. She'd really had quite enough of the ocean for the time being.

The river widened and shallowed. She swam toward the edge. A stand of trees blocked this part of the river from the city streets beyond. No one was around. Finally, she was having some good luck. With shaking legs, she lumbered out of the water.

Her nose caught the scent of something familiar. She looked up into Durniad's smiling face.

"Damn it."

A FEW HOURS LATER, they had her rebandaged, dressed in a trailing pearl-colored gown, and standing beside Durniad at an altar dedicated to a goddess Tahlia knew nothing about. A man droned on about commitment and care, and she rolled her eyes for the ninth time.

"Remember," Durniad whispered, his lips at her ear. "Smile and do as you're told and you'll live. If not, I'll hand you over to my guards. I like to watch."

"Classy." She drew away from him.

A sneer curled his lip. "Say one more word like that. I dare you." His voice was barely audible. He gripped her hand and attempted to crush her fingers.

He wasn't nearly as strong as he believed himself to be.

Well, the plan now was *murder*. She'd end this fool's life tonight in their wedding chamber and it would be a good deed done for anyone and everyone he'd ever met. Forget the human and Fae relations, screw the agreement between King Lysanael and the human high queen. Tahlia had had enough. She'd spit this monster like the pig that he was, then fight her way out of the fortress. Maybe Marius would show up at some point and help out. Maybe not. But no matter what, she wasn't giving in to this idiot.

# CHAPTER 30

# MARIUS

Ragewing flew over a forested stretch of land between Midhampton and the Witch's house. Marius breathed in the cool evening air. He turned to check Ragewing's bandaged tail. Some would think the injury wasn't as serious being near the end of his tail rather than higher up, but that wasn't true at all. The tip of a dragon's tail helped them cut the air and steer their way through the wind currents. Every part of Ragewing worked to make him deadly in the sky, able to turn tight arcs and whip around to fire on attackers. When one element of that flying system was disturbed, especially the tip of the tail, the dragon suffered in the area of agility, response time, and stamina.

Attempting to be more like Tahlia, Marius tried to think positively. Ragewing was flying steadily with no wobble or sense of pain through the bond. He was quiet, but he usually was. Nothing out of the ordinary there. He didn't speak to Marius unless he had something important to say. Marius respected that.

They soared over a cluster of sycamores that waved their branches in the gusty breeze.

*I smell a dragon.*

Marius's body coiled, ready to take action. *Where?* He wished he had more than just a couple of blades.

*I can't see him, but he's there. I sense his presence and his scent is reminiscent of the Gwerhune.*

That was King Lysanael's forest, the wood that lay south of Caer Du.

A dark shape materialized about one hundred yards away. Ragewing snarled and let out a warning shower of sparks. It was a forest dragon—black in color and capable of an invisibility glamour. On the dragon's back, Queen Revna lifted a hand in greeting.

"My lady queen!" Marius echoed the gesture and tapped Ragewing, asking him to land.

Ragewing and Arkyn, the queen's forest dragon, flew in descending circles until they landed in a small clearing dotted with gold and red mushrooms.

Ragewing bowed his head to the queen as Marius dismounted.

Marius bowed low. "To what do we owe this meeting, my queen?"

She hopped from her smaller dragon and gave him

a smile. Queen Revna's smiles were honestly a bit frightening. She had Berserker blood from Fjordbok and had worked as the human king's assassin before meeting Fae King Lysanael. It was a romantic story that even the cold-hearted could be swept up in.

The queen's ice-blue eyes studied him. "Please, stand, Commander Marius."

He did so, and Ragewing rested on his haunches beside him.

"Your contact from Midhampton sent a message via his trained raven. You've made a mess of this mission, you know."

"I apologize. It has been challenging to say the least. Durniad has taken Lady Tahlia captive." Marius kept his features blank, trying for professionalism even though he longed to tear the damned world apart for his mate.

Queen Revna's lip curled. She was human, so she had no fangs to bear, but she'd obviously picked up the mannerism from King Lysanael. "That man needs to die. I will go with you back to Midhampton and we'll use Arkyn's invisibility to enter the city. You are still in possession of the Crown of Minds, yes?"

Marius nodded and took the crown from where he'd buckled it onto the back of his belt. He offered it to her.

"No, you keep it," the queen said. "I'd rather not have something on my head that I can drop while fighting or flying. Being Fae, you have better reflexes than me. We can infiltrate the city, and while we remain invisible, we can use the crown to covertly retrieve Lady Tahlia. By the way, you're handling this with surprising self-control. Lys would be frothing."

Ragewing grumbled quietly and Marius set a hand on his side.

"Oh, I am internally frothing, my queen," Marius said. "Unless you order me not to, I will kill Durniad."

The queen's eyes softened as if she could empathize with his protective feelings. But only a former assassin would give him that look when chatting about murder.

"I'm fine with it," she said, "but you must make it look like a heart attack or an accident. And Lysanael can't know about it. He must be free of any responsibility of this mess due to the agreement."

"Understood."

"Lady Tahlia won't talk under duress, correct?" the queen asked. "She's been trained?"

"She has. And she is the bravest female I know."

The queen smiled, and this time it was less frightening and more a show of genuine approval. "She certainly impressed me when she faced that Greenflanked Terror."

Marius bowed his head. "I will pass on your praise when we have her safe with us."

"Do you know where they are holding her?"

"My only guess would be the fortress, but where within its walls, I don't know."

"What is your protocol in these cases?"

"The captured knight will attempt to reach open air to prepare for rescue. We aim for balconies, rooftops... That sort of thing."

Hands on hips, Queen Revna nodded. She tapped one finger against her hip, thinking. "All right. We fly toward the fortress. I've seen a map and shared it with Arkyn, so we should be good to go. We'll circle three times to seek her out. If we don't find her that way, we will land on the rooftop and come up with the next plan based on the level of security on the grounds."

It was wonderful having a queen that knew how to handle a situation such as this. Queen Revna was no spoiled royal, raised simply to dance and embroider. She was a warrior queen with a vicious and strategic mind.

"How close must Ragewing and I stay to Arkyn for the glamour to cover us?" he asked.

"If he's feeling strong, you're fine to fly beside us at a comfortable position. He's grown stronger with the care he's received in the time I've been queen. If he is injured, or if we continue on for over two hours, you'll need to be closer. Fly right beside, above, or below us as best you can." The queen leaned over to eye Ragewing's tail, and her brow knitted. "Is he injured?"

"Yes. Durniad has a ballista and a bolt nipped the

top end of his tail. He was bleeding pretty badly, but thankfully, the wound has clotted. He isn't at full strength or agility, but he's close to it."

*And I wouldn't let you do this without me,* Ragewing said into Marius's mind.

Marius glanced at Ragewing, who was giving him a loaded look that said *do not underestimate me.*

*Even wounded, you remain the most powerful dragon in the world, my friend.*

*Correct.*

Marius wanted to grin, but his heart ached too much for Tahlia, for the chance to eviscerate Durniad for daring to set a finger on her.

"A ballista? You mean a large crossbow-type weapon?" the queen asked.

"Aye, my queen."

Grimacing in Arkyn's direction, she sucked air through her teeth. "Hope you're ready for this, pal," she said to the black dragon.

Arkyn huffed and raised his head high as if insulted she would even ask. She rolled her eyes and rubbed the smooth scales under his chin.

"All right, I think we are good to move on," she said.

Marius's frustration and anxiety over Tahlia eased somewhat as they flew, fully invisible to all, toward Midhampton's walls. The heat of Ragewing's body and the familiar feel of riding the wind calmed and cleared Marius's head. Even though they were invisible, Marius could see the others as usual.

A fog rolled in from the direction of the ocean. The blanket of ghostly white reached them, blocking Queen Revna and Arkyn from view.

*Don't worry,* Ragewing said. *I have their scent. We remain within the boundary.*

The city appeared out of the night's fog like a beast waiting to spring. Not one, but three ballistae stood on the walls, bolts loaded into place and three men at each one. The weapon in the middle swiveled suddenly, turning so that it pointed over the city itself instead of at the forest.

They would have to watch for them from every aerial direction.

*We're coming, Tahlia.* Marius wished for the hundredth time that he could communicate with his mate the same way he could with Ragewing. *Hold on, little salty.*

# CHAPTER 31

# TAHLIA

Tahlia followed Durniad into his bedchamber. A massive bed with curtains occupied the far wall. A table stood to the left of the door, wine pitcher and goblets readied for them. Woven in yellows and blues, a circular carpet covered the wide floor planks. Beside the bed, three windows looked out on the courtyard. A downspout ran along the left side of the window that hung closest to the large bed.

The guards shut the bedchamber door, leaving Tahlia alone with Durniad. Yet another mistake on their part. The first error they'd made was allowing her to take a quiet moment in the feasting hall before the guests arrived after the ceremony. She'd stashed a nice little eating knife between her breasts.

Durniad faced the tray sitting on the side table. "Would you like a glass of wine, my bride?"

"So many glasses." Tahlia removed the elaborate veil Durniad's assigned handmaidens had braided into her hair. Tossing it onto the floor, she drew Durniad's attention away from her, then she pulled out the knife. Keeping her hand against her side—the side facing away from Durniad—she held the weapon flush against her wrist with the hilt in the palm of her hand.

Durniad turned and handed her some wine. She took it and drank it down in one go. The burn was lovely. He finished his, his gaze roaming about her face and body, then set both their glasses back on the tray.

"Do not fight me, Alanna."

"That isn't my name."

"I have decided it is." His tone was brusque. He appeared to have mastered his impatience since their earlier spat, but the pulsing vein on the side of his forehead said his calm wouldn't last. "This is all very simple. Do as I say, and you'll live as a queen. I will treat you with care and appreciation."

"As long as I go by the name you prefer," she said. If she could get him to rush her, his weight alone would help her pierce his chest or throat.

He sniffed and studied her face like he was trying to read her intentions. "And do exactly as I instruct. I won't bother you often. I am a busy man."

"Busy claiming titles and tyranting along the coastline?"

His eyes narrowed, and that vein grew even more pronounced. "I don't believe *tyranting* is a word."

"If you get to make up names, I get to make up verbs."

"Kiss me, my bride. Kiss me, and let your new life begin. Or you can try to stab me with that little knife of yours and die trying."

So he had noticed. Hmm. He didn't attempt to disarm her, so she decided to move the conversation for the moment.

"How are you going to get the crown back?" she asked. "Or do you not really need it?"

His face flushed, and the vein practically waved at Tahlia. *Ew.*

"I will make a plan to retrieve the crown from that monster as soon I as receive word from my allies. Tell me where he will take the crown and I'll see to it that you have free time every day to walk wherever you please."

"I assume he'll destroy the crown the moment he is able."

Some of Durniad's bravado slipped as his eyes bugged out. "What?"

"He's not like you."

"What do you mean?"

She shrugged, her heart beating quickly now. "He's not attempting to be a god."

"Then he's a fool."

"Who are your allies?" Steeling herself for what was about to happen, she worked to even her breathing.

Durniad drew his fingertips along Tahlia's collarbone. She fought the urge to puke the wine he'd given her right back at him. Maybe later.

"Well, Alanna, my allies are many. First, we have the Witch. Ah, I see you know of her. Of course you do. Yes, she is on my payroll. The Eelsmen are another ally in my pocket."

Tahlia swallowed a bitter taste on the back of her tongue. The Eelsmen were a group of northern pirates known for the way they used prisoners as bait for the midsized kraken they caught for prize money.

"I also have a group of wild Fae working for me in your Fae king's forest. They're just there to stir up trouble and cause distractions."

"I have bad news for you on that one."

He frowned and ran a finger down her arm, toward the hand holding the knife. "Explain."

Tahlia grimaced. "Unfortunately, we set them all on fire."

"You did what?"

"With our dragons. You do remember the dragon element to this whole equation, right?"

His face went purple, and his hands went for her throat. Bracing her feet firmly on the floor for balance, she jabbed the knife between his ribs. He dropped to the floor, gasping and yanking on her dress.

He tried to yell, but she had nipped him in the lung. "Guards! Please…"

"My name is Tahlia, you prickbrain," she said as she flipped the knife and dragged it across his throat.

The door burst open, and five guards spilled in. Tahlia turned and ran for the windows, wishing she wasn't wearing a damn dress even though it was actually very pretty.

One thought spun through her mind as she balled up the skirt of her dress and punched through the window glass. She'd killed yet another person and she was totally fine with it. She climbed out the window while the guards shouted and followed. Well, that bastard deserved death as much as the pillaging thieves in the Gwerhune and Ophelia had, and she wasn't about to waste any energy on being upset about spilling his blood.

# CHAPTER 32

# MARIUS

Marius glanced at Queen Revna and Arkyn. The evening fog swirled around the black dragon's wings and the tiled roofs they flew over.

*I realize we are unseen, but can they not hear us, rider?*

Ragewing tipped to the right to avoid clipping a pointed tower that appeared to have some ritual purpose. The humans were gathering at its base with candles and were singing in a melody that brought to mind promises and the length of a life.

They were singing of a bonding.

Marius's stomach turned and he squeezed his eyes shut. The city was celebrating the wedding of Durniad and Tahlia.

And suddenly, Marius felt as if he was a living flame, roaring heat rising from the tips of his toes to the tips of his pointed ears. There was no word for the level of this righteous anger. For this outrage. The way he felt could only be encapsulated in a tremendous warning snarl, a sound he could not make at the moment. He would ruin their covert entry and only lessen the chances he could rescue his mate.

*Breathe, rider,* Ragewing whispered into his mind. *We will have her with us soon and Durniad will be dead, his blood easing the pain in your soul.*

Marius wanted to thank Ragewing, but gratitude was as amorphous as the fog. He couldn't grasp it to pass it on and so he just held to his dragon and leaned into the fact that they were bonded and Ragewing knew exactly how Marius was feeling.

When they reached the fortress, Marius waved a hand at the queen and pointed to the structure. Bowers of dark greenery showed between the plumes of wispy cloud. The humans had decorated the structure for the wedding, stretching lengths of braided flowers and leafy branches from window to window. Banners of bright red matched the festival's last tomato remnants on the cobbled streets below. To think he and Tahlia had laughed together not that long ago. It felt like a lifetime had passed. Each moment she was inside that fortress with a male who believed himself mated to her was another lifetime again.

Damn this fog! He was fairly certain Tahlia wasn't

on any of the window balconies or on the roof. But could he be sure?

Queen Revna motioned for them to circle the rooftop again and Ragewing followed orders.

Marius shut his eyes and inhaled deeply, seeking his mate's beautiful scent, but it wasn't there. The fishy odor of the river, the refuse of a large population, and the soft aroma of the flowers and greenery were the only scents floating through the mist.

A crash sounded, glass catching the scant moonlight as it flew outward from an upper-floor window.

*There!* Marius shouted into Ragewing's mind. *Hold!*

Ragewing hovered and Arkyn did likewise beside them. A figure in a dress appeared on the downspout, then crawled over the lip of the roof to stand on the slant of rounded tiles.

Her scent was both a balm to Marius's heart and a fuel to the fire eating him alive.

Tahlia lifted her chin, looking for them. She slipped, her skirts flipped up on one side.

Marius's heart stopped.

As she tried to right herself, her foot shot out. She grabbed the tiles with a hand and stood again.

He exhaled, his head swimming. "Hold out your hand!" Marius shouted.

She started in surprise, then did as he asked, holding her arm out straight and bending her knees. Though she had to be wondering how they'd managed to be invisible, she knew what they would attempt.

Guards climbed the downspout as Tahlia had. They would be within reach of her in seconds.

*Go, please, as we have practiced,* Marius said to Ragewing.

The scent of blood rose in Marius's nostrils and he gritted his teeth. His mind was a whirlpool. He couldn't smooth the path of his thoughts.

Ragewing and Arkyn rose up, then swooped low to circle tightly around the fortress's roof.

Marius leaned as far as he was able down Ragewing's side, then he gripped Tahlia's upper arm while she took hold of his. He helped her scramble up behind him, and the sound of fabric ripping found his ears as she settled in the back section of the saddle.

"Whose blood is it?" He inhaled her scent.

"Take a guess," she whispered, her tone bright.

He smiled as the fire that had been consuming him eased into a delightful warmth. "Spoken like a seasoned Mist Knight." He reached down, grabbed one of her hands from his waist, then kissed her knuckles as they flew toward the city walls. "Whether King Lysanael agrees or not, you have done your human side a great favor in ridding this city of that vile soul."

She sat up suddenly, and the hair that had fallen from her intricate braids whipped forward in the chaotic wind from Ragewing's wings. He glanced at her. Her gaze was pinned to Queen Revna and Arkyn.

"Her dragon is the reason we are all invisible, right? Not a Witch's spell?"

"Yes. This is Arkyn's magic."

Lifting her shoulders, she wiggled, which did delightful albeit inconvenient things to his body. "How exciting!" She clamped her hand over her mouth.

They kept their voices quiet as they soared over the moonlit city. Though they couldn't be seen, they could still be heard.

"Before I escorted Durniad's sorry arse to the after-life," Tahlia murmured, "he claimed to be in league with the Witch herself as well as the Eelsmen."

"I seriously doubt the Witch would give him the time of day. But the Eelsmen..." He grunted, thinking. "We'll deal with them in the next moon. It matters little whom he was in league with anyway since he is gone."

"So are you finally finished loathing humans?"

The hesitation in her voice punched a hole in his heart. "I don't loathe everyone in Midhampton and I certainly don't loathe you."

She held him tightly, and her body moved as she took a deep breath. "Well, I am glad to hear my mate doesn't hate me."

The tear in his heart ripped open further. He took

her hand again and nipped at her palm. "You know what I mean." Gods, she smelled wonderful, and he couldn't wait to ravish her properly.

Through the plumes of mist, the ballistae on the city walls whipped around to face them. Those manning the weapons looked around like their heads were on swivels, so Marius was fairly certain they remained invisible.

Queen Revna eyed Marius and pointed up.

*Ragewing, prep for a launch.*

*On it.*

# CHAPTER 33

# TAHLIA

Ragewing shot toward the very moon itself and Tahlia nearly swallowed her brains. The queen's black dragon did likewise—the flying part, not the brain eating—assumably because remaining close kept them all invisible and they needed to get out of range of the ballistae. The cool night air bit at Tahlia's cheeks and she grinned widely, restraining herself from whooping with joy.

The dragons leveled out until the city was a fogged gathering of stone that appeared to be the size of a fisted hand. They flew quickly past the walls and over the nearby forest.

"We are visible now!" Queen Revna shouted over the wind, her words barely audible.

Tahlia knew how that felt. Their voices weren't powerful like Marius's and the other Mist Knights.

"To the Witch's abode, my lady queen?" Marius asked, using said Mistgold blood power.

She nodded, and the dragons flew onward into the night. Tahlia couldn't decide what was more exciting: Marius's divine body against hers—she shivered with delight as he gripped her thigh with one of his perfectly large hands; the success of their mission—if one didn't fret overmuch about the murdering; or the fact that the Witch was now responsible for healing Lija and soon she'd be in the skies with Tahlia, flying high and heading for battles with pirates.

"How much trouble will I be in for killing Durniad?"

"No more than Ragewing and I will be for exposing our identities."

"I hope we get to share a dungeon cell at least." Tahlia slid a hand over Marius's leg and stroked the inner side of his powerful thigh. Oooh, she loved those thighs.

Marius growled low in his throat, the sound he made when pleased but also not able to approve. It was one of her favorite sounds.

At the Witch's house, Ragewing and Arkyn landed. The queen remained on her dragon's back, but Marius dismounted and bowed. Tahlia followed, taking Marius's hand. An owl hooted from the peaked roof of the Witch's abode, and a chill ran over Tahlia's back. She ripped off the remainder of the dress's skirts, glad that she'd slipped some loose sleeping trousers underneath before she'd been "married" to Durniad.

Queen Revna cleared her throat and looked around, as if she was expecting someone. "Well, this is where I leave you. I was never here. You never saw me," the queen said quietly, and then she and her forest dragon flew away.

The branches of the oaks overhanging the Witch's house waved in the wind of Arkyn's wings. Marius looked at Tahlia; he was chewing the inside of his cheek as if deep in thought.

"What was that all about?" Tahlia whispered.

Marius grumbled. "She was helping us in an unofficial capacity, so we must pretend that she never did. We'll give the crown to the king. He doesn't need to know details."

He unbuckled his belt and handed her the crown. It was invisible in spots; the Witch's concoction was wearing off.

"But we will have to tell him that we killed Durniad, right?" She turned the crown over in her hands, studying its shine and weight. "And that the humans saw Ragewing."

"I suppose so," Marius said. "We wouldn't want to hold anything back that would come out later. They need to know a portion of the challenges we encountered and the changes in plan we were forced to enact."

As they approached the Witch's door, the heavy piece of oak and metal swung open on its own. Tahlia leaned around Marius to look at the strange blue lighting of the house as she trailed him inside. The Witch and King Lysanael stood at a cauldron in the center of the room. Sparks flicked from the black pot like little stars. Scary little stars.

Tahlia bowed and Marius joined her in the movement. The whole place smelled like danger, and it did absolutely nothing to soothe Tahlia's nerves.

Though this mission was over, it felt like a new one had already begun.

What would the king do when he found out that she and Marius had compromised information and pretty much negated the entire agreement? Could the king remove them from the order of the Mist Knights? Technically the king and queen were in charge of the order, even though he took little action in the day-to-day activities and lived far, far away from Dragon Tail Peak and the heart of the Mist Knights' operation. He could put them to death if he wanted to, but the king didn't seem like an unfair male.

Tahlia gulped and wiped sweating palms on her dress. She truly hoped her guess was accurate.

The Witch opened her mouth to speak, but King Lysanael cut her off. She gave him an irritated look, her eyebrows flicking together and her cloudy eyes darting left and right.

"Lady Tahlia," King Lysanael said, "I would like you to report in full what progressed in the city of Midhampton. I see that you have the crown."

Why was he asking her to report and not Marius? As Commander, Marius was the one responsible for reporting to the king. A thought shimmered through Tahlia's mind. Oh. It was the fact that she could lie. Though Queen Revna had acted as if the king knew nothing of their escapade, obviously the two were exchanging information of some sort. Perhaps the king was aware that some information would have to be altered or withheld. And so he had asked Tahlia, hoping she could do the job using the human half of her blood.

Hoping she was doing the right thing, she detailed most of the happenings, but left out pieces of the tale here and there to avoid angering the humans and the Witch who loved the human high queen like a daughter.

The back door of the Witch's house opened, and Tahlia thought Queen Revna had returned. But instead, a slight young girl who couldn't have been older than fifteen walked in. Behind her, a tall woman with silver-shot hair pulled tightly back and wrinkles at the edges of her eyes entered. This was the human high queen and her regent.

Marius inclined his head, not bowing as far as he did for King Lysanael, and Tahlia mimicked the movement. The Witch bowed to no one. The king nodded his head respectfully, a shallower nod than Marius's or Tahlia's.

"Thank you for saving my people," the young queen said.

Her voice was sweet with the newness of youth, but it was steady and strong and gave Tahlia the idea that someday she would be a good queen.

The regent merely pinched her lips together and glared at the king, Marius, and Tahlia in turn.

"And where is the crown?" the regent asked.

King Lysanael lifted it up. "Right here."

The regent's eyes glittered with the look of one plotting something unpleasant. "What are we planning to do with it?"

"Destroying it, as we discussed," the king said, his voice calm but packed with power.

Clasping her hands at her waist, the regent gave the young queen a simpering smile. "Are we sure that is the best course of action? With this crown, we could solve a great many of the world's problems."

"Could you?" the Witch asked, her voice haunting and quiet, though every ear heard it clearly, Tahlia was sure. Anytime the Witch spoke, it was like one had no choice but to listen.

The tension in the room increased so much that it

almost felt as though the air buzzed. She blew out a breath, wishing she could tell a joke to lighten the mood.

King Lysanael handed the crown to the Witch. "Destroy it. Now. As we all agreed." He looked over his shoulder at the young queen, ignoring the regent entirely.

"Yes," the young queen said, not a quaver in a single syllable.

Tahlia liked her very much. She smiled at the queen and gave her a nod. The queen grinned back.

The Witch held the crown over the cauldron. "I prepared its destruction. Now, stand back."

She dropped the crown into the steaming mixture. Bright, green light flashed and Tahlia winced, shutting her eyes. When she opened them, red stars filled the air—pinpricks of floating lights that for some reason she didn't want anywhere near her. She shifted her feet to avoid one that floated near her shoulder.

The Witch chanted sounds that were likely magic words and the red stars stilled. The stars shot toward the cauldron. A crack sounded from the bowl's steaming depths. Tahlia held her ears as they rang.

The Witch eyed the cauldron, which had stopped steaming and was only popping lightly. "It is done."

The regent blew air through her nostrils and turned away, her jaw set, while the young queen nodded approvingly.

"Thank you, Witch," King Lysanael said. He turned to face the queen. "Now, I must relay some changes my knights had to make to the plan."

Tahlia stood straight as the king detailed the appearance of Ragewing, the town's response, and then finally, how Tahlia had been forced to kill Durniad.

"I will consider whatever corrections you have in mind to rectify the peace in your town of Midhampton. How can I help?" the king said, crossing his arms and giving the young queen an encouraging look.

The regent whispered into the young queen's ear, but she was foolish if she didn't think King Lysanael and Marius couldn't hear every word. Tahlia couldn't quite catch the whole statement, but she heard her name in there along with *donation*.

Shaking her head, the queen looked up at King Lysanael. "I'm glad to be done with Durniad. I will simply address the city and declare that we had an agreement with your kingdom. There will be rebellion because of it. A knot of folks there are staunchly set against the Fae. But I will deal with that. You have done us a great service, and I'm glad your knights and your dragon, Ragewing, weren't mortally harmed in the completion of this mission."

"How did you get Lady Tahlia out of the city after the killing?" the regent asked, nearly cutting off her queen.

Marius's eyebrow lifted. "If I may, King Lysanael?" he asked, wanting permission to address the regent.

Tahlia bit her lip. How was this going to go? Gods, she was sweating. She was a damned fountain.

King Lysanael nodded. "Of course, Commander Marius."

Marius spread his hands wide, palms up. "We were the recipients of luck, really."

He couldn't lie. How was he going to keep Queen Revna and Arkyn out of this tale? Why had he offered to speak up?

"A thick fog rolled in that night. Ragewing and I used the cover to evade the ballistae. As my king explained, Lady Tahlia had escaped the guards and climbed to the roof. We simply picked her up and fled before the fog had completely lifted."

"Luck." The queen grinned and studied his face. "A great tale for the ages. I look forward to sharing it with my children someday."

The regent glared but held her tongue.

Tahlia exhaled. Ah, the deceit of simple omission. Of course, Marius was wise enough to keep it simple. She was, once again, so incredibly grateful for him. And for Queen Revna, Arkyn, and Ragewing. She didn't want to imagine what would have happened to her if she'd been stuck in Midhampton with Durniad's blood on her hands. His guards hadn't just been city guards. They were pirates playing roles and Tahlia knew exactly how rough pirates played from the tales Titus and Maiwenn had told her.

"Will you tell me about the city's defenses?" the queen asked, eyeing Marius.

Marius looked to King Lysanael, who nodded. "Well, they have at least four ballista machines..."

He went on about the weapons, approximate numbers of guards, details on the city walls, and so forth.

One thing they hadn't brought up was Durniad's claim that he was allied with the Witch and with the Eelsmen of the North. The Witch didn't even flinch at the news of Durniad dying, so Tahlia doubted he had been telling the truth. Perhaps he had only said it to see how Tahlia would react considering he knew the Witch had dealings with the Fae from time to time.

Should she bring it up? Probably not. She fiddled with her ripped skirts as she pondered. Why didn't more of her Mist Knight training involve how to handle reporting like this? What if she got Marius into trouble by not mentioning Durniad's supposed enemies? Maybe she should just interject. Marius was about finished. She didn't want King Lysanael to mistake their silence on this for any sort of treasonous behavior.

"Also," she began.

Marius looked at her, his usual scowl not giving anything away. She hoped this was the right move.

Tahlia cleared her throat. "Durniad claimed to have allies in the Eelsmen of the North. He said he was in league with the Witch, too."

Marius's face went very blank, as if he was hiding how he felt about her reporting these details.

King Lysanael's mouth parted as if in shock. He whirled to face the Witch. He didn't approach her. His movements were stilted as if he was plenty wary of the scary lady.

"Can you explain Durniad's suggestion of your involvement?" he asked her.

"You have no right to question our Witch," the regent snapped.

The young queen looked from the regent to King Lysanael, obviously unsure on what to do.

The ceiling flickered with blue light, almost like lightning. "Are you accusing me of being disloyal to my queen?"

"You sided with us against her father not so long ago," King Lysanael said.

Tahlia remembered a bit about that story, about how the Witch had hidden the young queen from her father, who at the time had been king. That tale was tied into the one about how Queen Revna had met King Lysanael.

"I did so to protect souls that the former king had in his grip. That situation had changed and your Druid tested the truth of my heart. You recall that day, I'm certain, King Lysanael."

"I do. I wish our Druid was here to mediate."

The great Fae magician was very ill, or so the gossip said. He had once helped the Realm of Lights with many great tasks.

The queen clasped her hands in front of her. A large seal ring on her thumb reflected the light of the scones on the walls. "Well, I trust the Witch, and Durniad is dead, so what does it matter?"

"I suppose it doesn't," the king said quietly. "I offer my apologies, Witch, for questioning your loyalty to your queen."

"Thank you." The Witch watched the king with her haunted eyes. Could she truly see in the way those with normal eyes did?

"As for the Eelsmen," Marius said, watching the rulers as if he wasn't certain he was permitted to speak, "they likely have every criminal on every coastline at least halfway in their gold-heavy pockets, so that's nothing shocking."

Everyone agreed, and the Witch stepped forward. "If you are prepared to travel, I will meet you at Dragon Tail Peak in two days' time."

Would Ragewing take the Witch on his back too?

The Witch's head turned toward Tahlia, and Tahlia swallowed.

"I will travel by way of a portal created only for my body," the Witch said.

"Ah, magic. Of course," Tahlia said, then she buttoned her lip. She hadn't meant to speak that out loud.

The young queen grinned at Tahlia. Tahlia rolled her eyes at herself, which made the queen laugh out loud.

Tahlia wished she could tell Lija that they would be home soon, and the Witch would be showing up in some surely fantastic manner forthwith.

The mission was finally over. Hopefully, Lija would be flying within the next few days.

# EPILOGUE

Tahlia

"Huzzah!" The hall echoed with the Mist Knights' cheers, the staff's praise, and the roar of the dragons gathered in the courtyard outside the open doors.

On the dais at the front of the hall, Fara and the two others who had tested alongside her raised the scrolls that named them official Healers of the Peak. Seated on one of the benches at the long, food-heavy tables, Tahlia shouted so ferociously that her throat burned. She didn't care. She couldn't have been happier.

*Lady Fara looks five feet taller,* Lija said into Tahlia's mind.

Tahlia turned on the bench to see Lija peering through the right-side doorway. *She does! Do you want one of these?* Tahlia lifted a pink crystal cake and wiggled it.

*You know that I do, rider.*

Tahlia chuckled. She jogged over to meet the dragon at the door. She held out the cake and Lija basically inhaled the sweet treat.

Marius stood beside Fara and Albus on the dais, his hands raised to quiet the chaos. "All right. That's enough. Now, eat the food you've been given and let's enjoy our pre-pirate raid rest period."

The crowd erupted in cheers once more. Plates and cups banged and clanked around the hall as toasts were made. Platters of rosemary roasted venison, pitchers of crystal wine, and deep bowls of noodles with cream sauce were passed from person to person.

Tahlia gave Lija a quick scratch under the chin, then returned to the benches to meet Fara for dining. Atticus was already there, as well as Enora and Justus. They toasted Fara again, also praising Tahlia for her secret mission work. Jokes were told, flirting commenced, and fun was had all around.

Fara gripped Tahlia's hand tightly. Her eyes shone with unshed tears. "Thank you for finishing up that secret mission nonsense and getting back here in time.”

“I wouldn’t have missed it for the world.”

“Unless you had contracted an ague or even the plague.” Fara’s face fell. “I forgot to ask. You did avoid drinking that human water, right?”

“Shh, you’re not supposed to know we were beyond the Veil.”

“Whatever. Tell me. I need to know.” Fara lifted Tahlia’s chin and examined her throat. “Your lymph nodes might be swollen.” She prodded her throat roughly and Tahlia coughed and pushed Fara’s hands away.

“Well, they are now anyway. Leave me alone. I’m perfectly fine.”

“Except for your weird Weaver scar.”

“It’s great actually. Now I’ll never lose the belt. It’s part of me.”

“Has your magic returned in full?”

“As of this morning. I think I just needed a good night’s rest inside the Veil’s range.”

Fara nodded, but her brow remained furrowed. “If you say so. But I think you should take some time with the crystals and Lija. We have yet to determine how much they can heal a Fae, but they do improve mental clarity and energy levels. We tested it!”

She shoved a sage-green cake into her mouth and

kept on talking. Titus, Ewan, Claudia, and Maiwenn found seats nearby. They began discussing the coming trip north.

"Tahlia, you ready for another adventure or do you need some more of Maiwenn's greenblood?"

Tahlia pretended to be choking. "Yeah, no. I'm good to go when it's time without any of that poison, thanks very much."

Titus snorted a laugh and began rolling dice while the others talked about potential pirate landing spots.

"Care for a midnight flight?" a deep voice said behind Tahlia.

She shivered with delight and turned to see Marius looking down at her with eyes that promised more than flying. He wore a black tunic that matched the inkings that peeked from the neckline and over one shoulder. His trousers were tucked into the soft boots he preferred when they weren't on a mission or train-ing, and he wore a braided belt with one small dagger sheathed near the brass buckle. Scowling, he tucked a hair behind her ear and she swallowed, heat already pooling low in her belly. His jaw flexed as he took her in, his gaze like a hand smoothing down the side of her neck to her breasts. Her body pulsed with want. Gods, the way he could affect her with just a look...

"Fara, I'll see you in the morning. All right?"

Fara nodded, waving an icing-covered hand at her, then continuing her line of questioning aimed at

Ewan. "But don't you think you need a Healer with your units?"

"You'll fall off during fighting."

"I'll show you falling off." Fara started toward Ewan, and Tahlia started to grab her arm to hold her back, but Maiwenn stepped in and snagged the back of Fara's tunic.

"I've got this, Tahl. Enjoy your time off," Maiwenn said.

Tahlia gave her a smile. "Thanks."

THE NIGHT WAS clear and absolutely bursting with stars. Lija spread her four wings wide and soared above Ragewing. Marius glanced up their way and Tahlia's heart sputtered as she imagined what might be going through his mind at the moment.

Lija made a content, rumbling sound deep in her belly, which vibrated through Tahlia.

*Ah. I'm finally myself again,* the dragon said into Tahlia's mind.

Tahlia leaned forward in the saddle and ran a hand down Lija's neck. *I'm so relieved. I was truly worried about you.*

*I was worried too.*

*It's brave of you to admit it.* Normally, dragons were too arrogant to be open about their feelings of vulnerability. It was a rare feeling for them in general, so they had little practice.

*That Witch stank of Unseelie power, but I can't say I'm not eternally grateful.*

Tahlia huffed a laugh. *I was glad to see her go. I don't think she likes Fae or dragons, honestly.*

*No, she does not. But at least she honored her word and healed me when others could not.*

*Agreed.*

*Ragewing said he would like to drop you and Commander Marius at the Starwing Cave while we fly over Goblin's Pass.*

*He always wants to see the most barren of places.*

Lija laughed. *He likes the dramatic vistas.*

*You don't mind?*

*No, because right after we're going to swim at Steaming Aspen.*

Steaming Aspen was a high mountain lake fed partially by hot springs, so it remained unfrozen year-round. *Oooh, that will be fun. You'll have to take me next time.*

*Will do, rider.*

Lija and Ragewing swooped low over the gray pebbles that marked the path up to Starwing Cave, a popular spot for mated Fae to visit on special evenings, and soon Marius and Tahlia were hand in hand on the ground.

They watched their dragons soar into the stars.

"She's doing very well. I'd have thought she'd be

too fatigued for such an adventure tonight," Marius said. His thumb rubbed the knuckle of her forefinger, and she felt like a fool with how the simple act made her cheeks heat.

"She's the best."

Marius chuckled in full then, a rare and lovely sound that she treasured.

"Is this your first time here?" he asked as they walked under a low arch of stone and into the cave.

It was oddly warm for a cave. She parted her lips to answer, but no sound came. The cave sparkled with teal, rose, and golden light.

"They're butterflies!"

The luminescent creatures fluttered along every inch of the rough stone walls, their light reflected in the occasional puddle of snowmelt.

"They come here to rest before finishing their migration south for the winter. The magma inside this peak runs close to the floor of this cave and so the area remains far warmer than the outside."

Tahlia let go of his hand and spun, taking it all in. "It's absolutely beautiful."

Marius walked ahead of her, then he stopped and gestured to a tumble of smooth rocks. Golden moss cloaked the ancient stones, and runes had been carved into the base of them.

"What is this all about?" She touched one of the runes and a shiver of magic danced up her arm. The threads she sometimes saw with her Weaver magic became clear, connecting the runes to one another, to the butterflies, and to Marius and her.

"They're blessing runes. Nothing too powerful, but set here long ago by the gods as a gift to Fae couples. Come," he said, holding out his hand.

She took it and he drew her to him as he sat on one of the mossy stones. She straddled him and bit her lip at how happy he already was to be here with her.

Shifting her hips, she pressed into him. A jolt of sheer pleasure made her gasp. "I see you have more than sightseeing on your mind, Commander."

He smoothed her hair away from her shoulders and began nibbling her neck. His body was so warm and her core pulsed with want.

"You are an astute observer, Lady of the Skies."

His tongue flicked over her collarbone, and he gripped her hips, easing her more firmly against him. He raised his hips and pleasure rode across Tahlia's center. She exhaled next to his ear and he snarled lightly into the space under her jaw.

"I want to see how little movement it takes to satisfy you," he said, his voice incredibly deep and gruff, as if he was having a difficult time controlling himself.

She was panting, and honestly, she didn't care how easily he aroused her. It was fantastic. "That's just mean," she said breathily, teasing.

He licked her throat in one great sweep, but he refused to move even as she wiggled in the vise of his hands on her hips. Again, he licked her—this time over the hollow in her throat while he growled possessively. The feeling of his tongue, his chest vibrating with his growling, and his cock so hard on her most sensitive spot were too much. She dug her fingers into his shoulders and rocked against him. Desire grabbed hold of her and shook her hard. Exquisite pleasure burst from her core, then outward.

"Now," she said, catching her breath and trembling, "this time you need to earn that."

He took a fistful of her tangled hair and chuckled into her temple. "As you say, my lady."

Drawing her tunic off, he dusted her with kiss after kiss. With slow and careful movements, he eased her onto her back. The moss was soft and smelled faintly sweet like jasmine and vanilla. She let him disrobe her completely, and once they were both unclothed, he lay on top of her and kissed her thoroughly. The way he moved his mouth over hers and how now and then he bit at her chin and lower lip with his fangs... Ah, it was perfection. She was swirling with desire, completely drunk with it by the time his hand slid down her stomach to cup her right where she wanted him to. His fingers knew exactly how to draw pleasure from her as he slowly increased the speed and enthusiasm of his stroking and pressing and rubbing. She was delirious with it and moaned his name, utterly out of her mind. He rose up on one elbow and entered her in one great rush. The fullness... It was the most glorious feeling.

"My lady of the skies," he whispered huskily against her forehead as he thrust forward hard.

Another explosion of pleasure built inside her and she grabbed at him to pull him closer, savoring the scent of him all around, everywhere.

He drove into her mercilessly and nipped at her breasts and brought forth an array of stunning sensations until she thought she would simply die right there of delight. But before she could come undone, he had her leg up high and had turned her onto her stomach, his body still linked with hers. She wasn't sure how they had even accomplished it, but she wasn't complaining.

"I love you, Tahlia," he said, his breath hot on the back of her neck as he thrust deeply inside of her. "I love you so very much." His body brushed along her back, their skin lightly sticking. "My soul aches with it."

She laced her fingers into his as he drove them toward ecstasy. "I love you, Marius. With everything I am."

"I love you exactly as you are," he said, and she knew he was talking about her human blood. "I would never change anything about you."

He could barely speak and she knew she couldn't

utter a word. The fullness of him and the way he knew exactly how to touch her here and there as he moved unstopping, never failing... The pleasure was more than she thought a person could experience. Her flesh went hot, and he sped up, and the world dissolved into a glittering, beautiful storm of their bond.

The threads around them shivered as Marius eased his way onto his side and curled himself around her. It was as if their love affected the magic as it did their hearts and souls.

"You were created to be my mate," he whispered into her ear as the butterflies glowed and sparkled around them and the sweet scent of the moss danced through the breeze. "I'm certain of that. And I was created for you."

She turned and cocooned herself into his massive body, delighting in the feel of his warm skin and the beat of his heart. "I thought I was only climbing the mountain to fly dragons. Lucky me, snagging a true mate in the process."

*Readers,*

*Thank you so much for joining Marius and Tahlia on another adventure! There will be one more book in this series, entitled Storm of Flames. It will be released in early*

2025. If you want to keep up with art reveals and bonus character interviews, join my newsletter at https://www.alishaklapheke.com/free-prequel-1.


THANKS,
   Alisha

# ACKNOWLEDGMENTS

I could never write a book without a freaking village of folks.

My family, for one. They put up with my spacey daydreaming and have eaten many a burned meals. They're all creative types too, so they inspire the heck out of me on the daily. Love you so very, very much.

My extended family. You are the sweetest bunch of people ever. You're always asking how the next book is going and then listening to me go on about elves, kissing, what exactly Fae are and aren't, why folklore is so cool, and so forth. You are so good at pretending it's interesting. Love you all.

My tribe, both online and in real life. NOFFA, Moontree, my local soul friends... You're all amazing. I would have long since been bald from tearing my hair out if it weren't for you. Thank you infinity.

My Dragon Divas are at many times the oxygen in my world. When I get overwhelmed or need love or cheering, they are ALWAYS there. I adore each and every one of you. Breathe fire, divas. Never accept anything but what you freaking deserve.

My Denners and Uncommon Crew, you all are the absolute best group of readers a gal could ask for. Seriously. I wish I could buy each and every one of you a dragon.

To my editor, designers, and artists—you complete me. Literally. Thank you so much for being so creative, flexible, and fabulous.

And to my cats. When I get stressed and lie prostrate on my yoga mat, you curl up beside me and lower my heart rate like the little gods and goddesses you are. I'm blessed to have your furry little arses in my life. Now, stop begging for treats. Seriously though.

# ABOUT THE AUTHOR

USA Today Bestselling Author Alisha Klapheke writes YA and NA fantasy and fantasy romance from her home just south of Nashville. She also teaches martial arts at her husband's dojo. When she isn't writing or teaching, you can find her in the woods. If she wants you to... (insert witch cackle here)

# Also by Alisha Klapheke

Bound by Dragons Series

Bound by Dragons

Kingdom of Spirits

Crown and Dragon

Book Four (tba)


Realm of Dragons and Fae Series

(standalones—read any in any order)

The Fae King's Assassin

The Unseelie King's Rebel

The Pirate King's Thief


Kingdoms of Lore Series

(standalones, more interconnected)

Enchanting the Elven Mage

(Sleeping Beauty retelling)

Enchanting the Fae Prince

(Robin Hood retelling)

Enchanting the Dragon Lord

(Beauty and the Beast retelling)

Stolen by the Shadow King

(Hades and Persephone retelling)

Rise of the Fire Queen

(continued)

Enchanting the Dryad Prince

(If Groot was hot...)

Dragons Rising Series

Fate of Dragons

Band of Breakers

Queen of Seas

Sword of Oak

Magic of Lore

(this series is set in the same world as Kingdoms of Lore but 1000 years earlier)

The Edinburgh Seer Trilogy

The Edinburgh Seer

The Edinburgh Heir

The Edinburgh Fate

Queens of Steel and Starlight/Uncommon World Series

(standalones that interconnect in last book so be sure to read these in order)

Waters of Salt and Sin

Fever (connecting novella)

Plains of Sand and Steel

Forest of Silver and Secrets

Rune Kingdom